Horatio Alger

Tony the Hero

A brave boy's adventures with a tramp

Horatio Alger

Tony the Hero
A brave boy's adventures with a tramp

ISBN/EAN: 9783337194444

Printed in Europe, USA, Canada, Australia, Japan

Cover: Foto ©Andreas Hilbeck / pixelio.de

More available books at **www.hansebooks.com**

Tony set to work with rapid hands to tie the prostrate tramp hand and foot.—(See page 73.)

2

—OR,—

A Brave Boy's Adventures With a Tramp.

By HORATIO ALGER, Jr.,

Author of

"Tom, the Bootblack;" "Joe's Luck;" "Frank Fowler, the Cash Boy;"
"Tom Temple's Career;" "Tom Thatcher's Fortune;"
"The Errand Boy," etc., etc.

ILLUSTRATED.

NEW YORK:
A. L. BURT. PUBLISHER.

TONY, THE HERO.

——◆——

CHAPTER I.

THE TWO WANDERERS.

A MAN and a boy were ascending a steep street in a country town in Eastern New York. The man was tall and dark-complexioned, with a sinister look which of itself excited distrust. He wore a slouch hat, which, coming down over his forehead, nearly concealed from view his low, receding brow. A pair of black, piercing eyes looked out from beneath the brim. The first impression produced upon those who met him was that he was of gipsy blood, and the impression was a correct one. Where he was born no one seemed to know; perhaps he did not himself know, for all his life he had been a wanderer, but English was the tongue that he spoke, and, apart from the gipsy dialect, he knew no other.

His companion was a boy of fourteen. Between the two there was not the slightest resemblance. Though embrowned by exposure to the sun and the wind, it was easy to see that the boy was originally of light complexion. His hair was

chestnut and his eyes blue. His features were regular and strikingly handsome, though, owing to the
vagrant life he was compelled to lead, he was not
able to pay that attention to cleanliness which he
might have done if he had had a settled home.

It was five o'clock in the afternoon, and the boy
looked weary. He seemed scarcely able to drag one
foot after the other. His companion turned upon
him roughly.

"What are you dawdling that way for, Tony?"
he demanded. "You creep like a boy of three."

"I can't help it, Rudolph," said the boy, wearily;
"I'm tired."

"What business have you to be tired?"

"I've walked far to-day."

"You've walked no farther than I. I don't daw-
dle like you."

"You're a man. You're stronger than I am, Rudolph."

"And you're a milksop," said the man contemptuously.

"I'm nothing of the sort," said the boy, with a
flash of spirit. "I'm not made of cast-iron, and
that's why I can't stand walking all day long. Besides, I have had no dinner."

"That isn't my fault, is it?"

"I didn't say it was, but it makes me weak for
all that."

"Well," said Rudolph, "perhaps you're right. I
feel like eating something myself. We'll go to some
house and ask for supper."

Tony looked dissatisfied.

"I wish we were not obliged to beg our meals," he said; "I don't like it."

"Oh, you're getting proud, are you?" sneered Rudolph. "If you've got money to pay for your supper, we won't beg, as you call it."

"Why can't we do as other people do?" asked Tony.

"What's that?"

"Live somewhere, and not go tramping round the country all the time. It would be a good deal pleasanter."

"Not for me. I'm a vagrant by nature. I can't be cooped up in one place. I should die of stagnation. I come of a roving stock. My mother and father before me were rovers, and I follow in their steps."

The man spoke with animation, his eye flashing as he gazed about him, and unconsciously quickened his pace.

"Then, I'm not like you," said Tony, decidedly. "I don't want to be a tramp. Were my father and mother rovers like yours?"

"Of course they were," answered Rudolph, but not without hesitation. "Ain't I your uncle?"

"I don't know. Are you?" returned Tony, searchingly.

"Haven't I told you so a hundred times?" demanded Rudolph, impatiently.

"Yes," said the boy, slowly, "but there's no likeness between us. You're dark and I am light."

"That proves nothing," said the elder tramp, hastily. "Brothers are often as unlike. Perhaps you don't want to look upon me as a relation?"

The boy was silent.

"Are you getting ashamed of me?" demanded Rudolph, in a harsh tone.

"I am ashamed of myself," said Tony, bitterly. "I'm nothing but a tramp, begging my bread from door to door, sleeping in barns, outhouses, in the fields, anywhere I can. I'm as ignorant as a boy of eight. I can just read and that's all."

"You know as much I do."

"That don't satisfy me. When I grow up I don't want to be——"

Tony hesitated.

"You don't want to be like me. Is that it?" asked Rudolph, angrily.

"No, I don't want to be like you," answered Tony, boldly. "I want to have a home, and a business, and to live like other people."

"Humph!" muttered Rudolph, fixing his eyes thoughtfully upon his young companion. "This is something new. You never talked like that before."

"But I've felt like that plenty of times. I'm tired of being a tramp."

"Then you're a fool. There's no life so free and independent. You can go where you please, with no one to order you here nor there, the scene changing always, instead of being obliged to look always upon the same people and the same fields."

"What's the good of it all? I'm tired of it. I've got no home, and never had any."

"You've got no spirit. You're only fit for a farm-boy or an apprentice."

"I wish I was either one."

"Sit down here if you are tired," said the man, abruptly, throwing himself down under a wide-spreading tree by the roadside.

Tony stretched himself out at a little distance, and uttered a sigh of relief as he found himself permitted to rest.

"Have you been thinking of this long?" asked Rudolph.

"Of what?"

"Of not liking to be a tramp?"

"Yes."

"You have not spoken of it before."

"I've been thinking of it more lately."

"How did that come?"

"I'll tell you," said Tony. "Don't you remember last week when we passed by a school house? It was recess, and the boys were out at play. While you were away a few minutes, one of the boys sat down by me and talked. He told me what he was studying, and what he was going to do when he got older, and then he asked me about myself."

"What did you tell him?"

"What did I tell him?" said Tony, bitterly. "I told him that I was a tramp, and that when I got older I should be a tramp still."

"Well," said Rudolph, sharply, "what then?"

"The boy told me I ought to get some regular work to do, and grow into a respectable member of society. He said that his father would help me, he thought; and——"

"So you want to leave me, do you?" demanded Rudolph, fiercely. "Is that what you're coming to, my chicken?"

"It isn't that so much as the life you make me lead. I want to leave that, Rudolph."

"Well, you can't do it," said the man, shortly.

"Why not?"

"I say so, and that's enough."

Tony was silent for a moment. He was not greatly disappointed, for he expected a refusal. He changed the subject.

"Rudolph," he said, "there's something else I want to ask you about."

"Well?"

"Who am I?"

"Who are you? A young fool," muttered the tramp, but he appeared a little uneasy at the question.

"I want to know something about my father and mother."

"Your mother was my sister. She died soon after you were born."

"And my father?"

"He was put in jail for theft, and was shot in trying to make his escape. Does that satisfy you?"

"No, it doesn't, and what's more, I don't believe it," said Tony, boldly.

"Look here," said Rudolph, sternly. "I've had enough of your insolence. Do you see this strap?"

He produced a long leather strap, which he drew through his fingers menacingly.

"Yes, I see it."

"You'll feel it if you ain't careful. Now get up. It's time to be moving."

CHAPTER II.

THE FARM-HOUSE.

"WHERE are we going to stop to-night?" asked Tony ten minutes later.

"There," answered Rudolph, pointing out a farm-house, a little to the left.

"Suppose they won't let us."

"They will admit us into their barn, at least, if we play our cards right. Listen to what I say. You are to be my son."

"But I am not your son."

"Be silent!" said the other tramp, "and don't you dare to contradict me. You have been sick, and are too weak to go farther."

"That is a lie, Rudolph."

"That doesn't matter. If they believe it, they won't turn us away. Perhaps they will let you sleep in the house."

"Away from you?"

"Yes."

Tony was puzzled. It seemed as if Rudolph wanted him to be more comfortably provided for than himself, but the boy knew him too well not to suspect that there was some concealed motive for this apparent kindness.

"Well, what are you thinking about?" demanded Rudolph, suspiciously, as he observed the boy's earnest gaze.

"Why do you want me to sleep in the house?" he asked.

"I will tell you. When all the family are asleep, I want you to steal down stairs, open the back door, and let me in."

"What for?" asked the boy, startled.

"Never you mind. Do as I tell you!"

"But I don't want to do it. You never asked me to do that before."

"Didn't I? Well, I had no occasion. I ask you now;"

"What are you going to do? Are you going to harm any one?"

"No. I'll tell you what I'm going to do, but mind you, if you breathe a word to any being, I'll cut your tongue out."

Tony looked troubled, but not frightened.

"Go on," he said.

Rudolph continued in a rapid tone.

"I want money to carry out a plan of importance. This farm belongs to a farmer who is rich, and who keeps a part of his money in the house."

"How do you know that?"

"A friend of mine stopped there last week, and found out. He put me on the scent. The old man keeps from two to three hundred dollars in his desk. I must have that money."

"I don't want to help you in this, Rudolph," said Tony. I won't betray you, but you mustn't compel me to be a thief."

"I can't get along without you, and help me you must."

" Suppose we fail?"

"Then we must take to our legs. If we're caught we're both in the same box. I don't ask you to take any risk that I don't run myself."

Tony was about to remonstrate further, but it was too late. They had already reached the farm house, and caught sight of the owner standing under a tree in the front yard.

" Remember!" hissed the older tramp. " Follow my lead, or I'll beat you till you are half dead. Good evening, sir."

This last was said in a humble tone to the farmer, who advanced to the gate.

"Good evening," said the farmer, ingeniously.

He was a man of sixty, roughly dressed to suit his work, with grizzled hair, a form somewhat bowed, and a face seamed with wrinkles. He had been a hard worker, and showed abundant traces of it in his appearance.

"We are very tired and hungry, my boy and I," whined Rudolph. "We've traveled many miles since morning. Would you kindly give us some supper and a night's lodging?"

"My wife'll give you something to eat," said the old man. "Thank Heaven! we've got enough for ourselves and a bit for the poor besides. But I don't know about lodging. I don't like to take in strangers that I know nothing about."

"I don't blame you, sir," said Rudolph, in a tone of affected humility. "There's many rogues going round the country, I've heard, but I'm a poor, hard-working man."

"Then why are you not at work?"

"Times are hard, and I can get nothing to do. I am in search of work. I can do almost anything. I'm a carpenter by trade."

Rudolph knew no more of the carpenter's trade than the man in the moon, but that would do as well as any other.

"Where are you from?"

"From Buffalo," he answered, with slight hesitation.

"Is business dull there?"

"Nothing doing."

"Well, my friend, you haven't come to the right place. There's nothing but farming done here."

"I don't know anything about that," said Rudolph, hastily, for he had no disposition to be set to work in the fields.

"I don't need any extra hands," said the farmer.

"I am glad of that," thought the tramp.

"Go round to the back door, and I will speak to my wife about supper," said the old man.

"Come, Tony," said Rudolph, motioning to take the boy's hand, but Tony did not see fit to notice the movement, and walked in silence by his side.

A motherly-looking old woman made her appearance at the back door.

"Come in," she said. "Come right in, and sit down to the table. Abner, make room for the poor man and his son."

Abner was a stalwart youth of eighteen, hard-handed and muscular. He was the only permanent "hired man" employed on the farm. In haying time there were others transiently employed.

A farmer's table is plentiful, though homely. The two tramps made an abundant meal, both doing justice to the homely fare. The farmer's wife looked on with hospitable satisfaction. She could not bear to have anybody hungry under her roof.

"You'll excuse our appetite, ma'am," said Rudolph, "but we've had nothing to eat since breakfast."

"Eat as much as you like," said she. "We never stint anybody here. Is that your son?"

"Yes, ma'am."

Tony bent his eyes upon his plate, and frowned slightly. He wanted to deny it, but did not dare.

"He don't look a bit like you," said the woman. "He's light, and you're very dark."

"His mother was light," said Rudolph. "He takes after her."

"How old is he?"

"Tony, tell the lady how old you are."

"Fourteen."

"He is well grown of his age."

"Yes; he will make a good-sized man. He's been sick."

"Has he? What has been the matter?"

"I don't know. Poor folks like us can't call in a doctor."

"He don't look sick," said the farmer's wife, thoughtfully.

"He's delicate, though he don't look it. It's sleeping out in the open air, I expect."

" Do you have to sleep out in the open air?"

" Yes; we can't afford to pay for lodgings, and people won't take us into their houses. I don't mind myself—I'm tough—but Tony can't stand it as well as I can."

While this conversation was going on, Tony fixed his eyes upon his plate. He was annoyed to have such falsehoods told about him; but if he should utter a word of objection he knew there would be an explosion of wrath on the part of his guardian, and he remained silent.

The farmer's wife was a simple-minded, kind-hearted woman, and though Tony did not look at all delicate, she never thought of questioning the statement of Rudolph. Indeed she was already revolving in her mind inviting the boy to sleep in the house. She was rather prejudiced in favor of Rudolph by his show of parental solicitude.

When supper was over, having in the meantime consulted her husband, she said to Rudolph:

" My husband says you may sleep in the barn, if you don't smoke. We can find a bed for your son with Abner. You won't mind taking him into your room?"

" He can come," said Abner, good-naturedly.

So it was arranged. At half-past eight, for they retired at that early hour in the farm house, Rudolph left the fireside, and sought the barn. As he left the room he looked suspiciously at Tony, and shook his head warningly.

CHAPTER III.

RUDOLPH'S DISAPPOINTMENT.

ABNER slept in a large room in the attic. It had been roughly partitioned off, and was not even plastered. The beams were plainly visible. Upon nails which had been driven into them hung Abner's limited wardrobe. There were two cot-beds in the room, as a part of the year the farmer employed more than one hired man.

"You can sleep there, youngster," said Abner, pointing to one of the beds. "This is my bed."

"Thank you," said Tony, politely.

"I s'pose you've traveled round considerable," said Abner, with curiosity.

"Yes, a good deal."

"Do you like it?"

"No; I'm tired of it."

"How do you make your livin'?"

"As we can. We often go hungry."

"Why don't your father settle down somewhere?"

Tony thought of disclaiming the relationship implied, but he reflected that Rudolph would be angry, and merely answered:

"He prefers to travel round."

"Was you ever in New York?" asked Abner.

"Do you mean the city of New York? Yes."

"I'd like to see it," said Abner, regarding Tony

with new respect. "I've heard a sight about it. It's powerful big, isn't it?"

"It's very large."

"There's as many as a thousand houses, isn't there?"

"There's a hundred thousand, I should think," answered Tony.

"Sho? you don't say so!" exclaimed Abner, awe-struck. "I'd like to go there."

"Didn't you ever visit the city?"

"No; I never traveled any. I never was more'n fifteen miles from home. Dad wouldn't let me. When I'm a man, I'm bound to see the world."

"Ain't you a man now?" inquired Tony, survey-ing his Herculean proportions with astonishment.

"No; I'm only eighteen."

"You're as big as a man."

"Yes, I'm pooty big," said Abner, with a compla-cent grin. "I can do a man's work."

"I should think you might. I thought you were more than four years older than me. I'm fourteen."

"I guess I weigh twice as much as you."

"I'm not small of my age," said Tony, jealously.

"Maybe not. I'm a regular bouncer. That's what dad says. Why, I'm half as big again as he is."

"Does he ever lick you?" asked Tony, smiling.

"I'd like to see him try it," said Abner, bursting into a roar of laughter. "He'd have to get upon a milkin' stool. Does your dad lick you?"

"No," answered Tony, shortly.

"He looks as if he might sometimes.   He's kinder fractious-looking."

Tony did not care to say much on the subject of Rudolph.   He felt that it was his policy to be silent. If he said anything he might say too much, and if it got to Rudolph's ears, the man's vindictive temper would make it dangerous for him.

"We get along pretty well," he said, guardedly. "Do you get up early?"

"Four o'clock.   You won't have to, though."

"What time do you get breakfast?"

"Half-past five, after I've milked and done the chores.   You must be up by that time, or you won't get anything to eat."

"That's pretty early," thought Tony.   "I don't see the use of getting up so early."

"I guess I'll go to sleep," said Abner.   "I'm tuckered out."

"Good-night, then," said Tony.

"Good-night."

The young giant turned over, closed his eyes, and in five minutes was asleep.

Tony did not compose himself to sleep so readily, partly because Abner began to snore in a boisterous manner, partly because he felt disturbed by the thought of the treachery which Rudolph required at his hands.

Tony was only a tramp, but he had an instinct of honor in him.   In the farm house he had been kindly treated and hospitably entertained.   He felt that it would be very mean to steal down in the dead of night and open the door to his companion in order that he might rob the unsuspecting farmer of his money. On the other hand, if he did not do this, he knew that he would be severely beaten by Rudolph.

"Why am I tied to this man?" he thought. "What chance is there of my ever being anything but a tramp while I stay with him?"

He had thought this before now, but the circumstances in which he now found himself placed made the feeling stronger. He had been often humiliated by being forced to beg from door to door, by the thought that he was a vagrant, and the companion of a vagrant, but he had not been urged to actual crime until now. He knew enough to be aware that he ran the risk of arrest and imprisonment if he obeyed Rudolph. On the other hand, if he refused, he was sure of a beating.

What should he do?

It was certainly a difficult question to decide, and Tony debated it in his own mind for some time. Finally he came to a determination. Rudolph might beat him, but he would not be guilty of this treachery.

He felt better after he had come to this resolve, and the burden being now off his mind, he composed himself to sleep.

He did not know how long he slept, but he had a troubled dream. He thought that in compliance with his companion's order he rose and opened the door to him. While Rudolph was opening the farmer's desk, he thought that heavy steps were heard, and Abner and the farmer entered the room, provided with a lantern. He thought that Rudolph and himself were overpowered and bound. Just as he reached this part he awaked, and was reassured by hearing Abner's heavy breathing.

"I'm glad it's a dream," he thought, breathing a sigh of relief.

At this instant his attention was called by a noise upon the panes of the only window in the room.

He listened, and detected the cause.

Some one was throwing gravel stones against it.

"It's Rudolph!" he thought instantly. "He's trying to call my attention."

He thought of pretending to be asleep, and taking no notice of the signal. But he feared Abner would awake, and ascertain the meaning of it. He decided to go to the window, show himself, and stop the noise if he could.

He rose from his bed, and presented himself at the window. Looking down, he saw the dark figure of Rudolph leaning against the well-curb, with his eyes fixed on the window.

"Oh, you're there at last," growled Rudolph. "I thought I'd never wake you up. Is the man asleep?"

"Yes," said Tony.

"Then come down and let me in."

"I would rather not," said Tony, uneasily.

"What's the fool afraid of?" answered Rudolph, in a low, menacing tone.

"The man might wake up."

"No danger. Such animals always sleep heavily. There's no danger, I tell you."

"I don't want to do it," said Tony. "It would be mean. They've treated me well, and I don't want to help rob them."

"Curse the young idiot!" exclaimed Rudolph, in low tones of concentrated passion. "Do you mean to disobey me?"

"I can't do as you wish, Rudolph. Ask me anything else."

"I wish I could get at him!" muttered Rudolph, between his teeth. "He never dared to disobey me before. Once more! Will you open the door to me?" demanded Rudolph.

Tony bethought himself of an expedient. He might pretend that Abner was waking up.

"Hush!" he said, in feigned alarm. "The man is waking up. Get out of sight quick."

He disappeared from the window, and Rudolph, supposing there was really danger of detection, hurriedly stole away to the barn where he had been permitted to lodge.

He came out half an hour later, and again made the old signal, but this time Tony did not show himself. He had made up his mind not to comply with the elder tramp's demands, and it would do no good to argue the point.

"I wish I knew whether he was asleep, or only pretending, the young rascal," muttered Rudolph. "I must manage to have him stay here another night. That money must and shall be mine, and he shall help to get it for me."

CHAPTER IV.

SETTING A TRAP.

AT half-past five Tony got up. He would have liked to remain in bed two hours longer, but there was no chance for late resting at the farm house. Rudolph, too, was awakened by Abner, and the two tramps took their seats at the breakfast table with the rest of the family.

Rudolph furtively scowled at Tony. To him he attributed the failure of his plans the night before, and he was furious against him—the more so that he did not dare to say anything in presence of the farmer's family.

"Where are you going to-day?" asked the farmer, addressing Rudolph.

"I am going to walk to Crampton. I may get employment there."

"It is twelve miles away. That's a good walk."

"I don't mind it for myself. I mind it for my son," said Rudolph, hypocritically.

"He can stay here till you come back," said the farmer, hospitably.

"If you're willing to have him, I will leave him for one more night," said Rudolph. "It'll do him good to rest."

"He can stay as well as not," said the farmer. "When are you coming back?"

"Perhaps to-night, but I think not till to-mor-row."

"Don't trouble yourself about your son. He will be safe here."

"You are very kind," said the elder tramp. "Tony, thank these good people for their kindness to you."

"I do thank them," said Tony, glancing uneasily at the other.

When breakfast was over, Rudolph took his hat, and said:

"I'll get started early. I've a long walk before me."

Tony sat still, hoping that he would not be called upon to join him. But he was destined to be disappointed.

"Come and walk a piece with me, Tony," said Rudolph.

Reluctantly Tony got his hat, and set out with him.

As long as they were in sight and hearing, Rudolph spoke to him gently, but when they were far enough for him to throw off the mask safely, he turned furiously upon the boy.

"Now, you young rascal," he said, roughly, "tell me why you didn't obey me last night."

"It wasn't safe," said Tony. "We should both have been caught."

"Why should we? Wasn't the man asleep?"

"He stirred in his sleep. If I had moved about much, or opened the door, it would have waked him up."

"You are a coward," sneered Rudolph. "When I was of your age, I wouldn't have given up a job so easily. Such men sleep sound. No matter if they do move about, they won't wake up. If you had had a little more courage, we should have succeeded last night in capturing the money."

"I wish you'd give it up, Rudolph," said Tony, earnestly.

"You don't know what you're talking about," said the tramp, harshly. "You're a milksop. The world owes us a living, and we must call for it."

"I'd rather work than steal."

"There's no work to be had, and we must have money. More depends on it than you think. But we've got one more night to work in."

"What do you mean to do?" asked Tony, uneasily.

"Thanks to my management, you will sleep in the same room to-night. Look round the house during the day; see if the key's in the desk. If you can get hold of the money, all the better. In that case, come and hide it in that hollow tree, and we can secure it after the hue and cry is over. Do you hear?"

"Yes."

"But, if there is no chance of that, look out for me at midnight. I will throw gravel against your window as a signal. When you hear it, steal down stairs, with your shoes in your hands, and open the door to me. I will attend to the rest. And mind," he added, sternly, "I shall take no excuses."

"Suppose I am caught going down stairs?"

"Say you are taken sick. It will be easy enough to make an excuse."

"Are you going to Crampton?" asked Tony.

"Of course not. Do you think I am such a fool as to take a long walk like that?"

"You said you were going."

"Only to put them off the scent. I shall hide in yonder wood till night. Then I will find my way back to the farmhouse."

"Do you want me to go any farther with you?"

"No; you can go back now if you want to. Don't forget my directions."

"I will remember them," said Tony, quietly.

The two parted company, and Tony walked slowly back to the farm. He was troubled and perplexed. He was in a dilemma, and how to get out of it he did not know.

It was not the first time that he thought over his relations to Rudolph.

As far back as he could remember he had been under the care of this man. Sometimes the latter had been away for months, leaving him in the charge of a woman whose appearance indicated that she also was of Gipsy descent. He had experienced hunger, cold, neglect, but had lived through them all, tolerably contented. Now, however, he saw that Rudolph intended to make a criminal of him, and he was disposed to rebel. That his guardian was himself a thief, he had reason to know. He suspected that some of his periodical absences were spent in prison walls. Would he be content to follow his example?

Tony answered unhesitatingly, "No." Whatever the consequences might be, he would make a stand there. He had reason to fear violence, but that was better than arrest and imprisonment. If matters came to the worst, he would run away.

When he had come to a decision he felt better. He returned to the farm and found Abner just leaving the yard with a hoe in his hand.

"Where are you going?" he asked.

"To the corn field."

"May I go with you?"

"If you want to."

So Tony went out to the field with the stalwart "hired man," and kept him company through the forenoon.

"That's easy work," said Tony, after a while.

"Do you think you can do it?"

"Let me try."

Tony succeeded tolerably well, but he could not get over the ground so fast as Abner.

"Why don't you hire out on a farm?" asked Abner, as he took back the hoe.

"I would if I could," answered Tony.

"Why can't you? Won't your father let you?"

"He wants me to go round with him," answered Tony

"Wouldn't he take me instead of you?" asked Abner, grinning. I'd like to travel round and see the world. You could stay here and do farm work."

"If he and the farmer agree to the change, I will," answered Tony, with a smile.

At noon they went back to the farm house to dinner. Tony stared with astonishment at the quantity of food Abner made away with. He concluded that farm work was favorable to the appetite.

The afternoon passed rapidly away, and night came. Again Tony went up into the attic to share Abner's room. He got nervous as the night wore on. He knew what was expected of him, and he shrank from Rudolph's anger. He tried to go to sleep, but could not.

At last the expected signal came. There was a rattling of gravel stones upon the window.

"Shall I lie here and take no notice?" thought Tony.

In this case Rudolph would continue to fling gravel stones, and Abner might wake up. He decided to go to the window and announce his determination.

When Rudolph saw him appear at the window, he called out:

"Come down quick, and open the door."

"I would rather not," answered Tony.

"You must!" exclaimed Rudolph, with a terrible oath. "If you dare to refuse, I'll flay you alive."

"I can't do it," said Tony, pale but resolute. "You have no right to ask it of me."

Just then Tony was startled by a voice from the bed:

"Is that your father? What does he want?"

"I would rather not tell," said Tony.

"You must!" said Abner, sternly.

"He wants me to open the door and let him into the house," Tony confessed, reluctantly.

"What for?"

"He wants to get your master's money."

"Ho, ho!" said Abner. "Well, we'll go down and let him in."

"What!" exclaimed Tony, in surprise.

"Call from the window that you will be down directly."

"I don't want to get him into trouble."

"You must, or I shall think you are a thief, too."

Thus constrained, Tony called out that he would come down at once.

"I thought you'd think better of it," muttered Rudolph. "Hurry down, and waste no time."

Five minutes later, Abner and Tony crept down stairs, the former armed with a tough oak stick.

CHAPTER V.

AN ATTEMPT AT BURGLARY.

Unsuspicious of danger, Rudolph took a position on the door-step. He was incensed with Tony for having given him so much unnecessary trouble, and he was resolved to give the boy a lesson.

It was quite dark in the shadow of the house, and when the door opened, Rudolph, supposing, of course, it was Tony who had opened it, seized the person, whom he saw but dimly, by the arm, exclaiming venomously, as he tried to reach him:

"I'll teach you to keep me waiting, you young rascal."

He was not long in finding out his mistake.

Abner was considerably larger and more muscular than the tramp, and he returned the compliment by shaking off Rudolph's grasp, and seizing him in his own vise-like grasp.

"You'll teach me, will you, you villain," retorted Abner. "I'll teach you to come here like a thief."

"Let go," exclaimed the tramp, as he felt himself shaken roughly.

"Not till I've given you a good drubbing," returned Abner, and he began to use his cudgel with effect on the back and shoulders of the tramp. "You've come to the wrong house, you have."

Rudolph ground his teeth with ineffectual rage.

He lamented that he had not a knife or pistol with
him, but he had made so sure of easy entrance into
the house, and no resistance, that he had not pre-
pared himself.   As to brute force, he was no match
for Abner.

"The boy betrayed me! " he shrieked. " I'll have
his life."

" Not much," said Abner.   " You'll be lucky to
get away with your own.   It isn't the boy.   I was
awake, and heard you ask him to let you in.   Now
take yourself off."

As he said this he gave a powerful push, and Rudolph reeled a moment and sank upon the ground,
striking his head with violence.

"He won't try it again," said Abner, as he shut
to the door and bolted it.   "I guess he's got enough
for once."

Tony stood by, ashamed and mortified.   He was
afraid Abner would class him with the tramp who had
just been ignominiously expelled from the house.
He was afraid he, too, would be thrust out of doors,
in which case he would be exposed to brutal treatment from Rudolph.   But he did not need to fear
this.   Abner had seen and heard enough to feel convinced that Tony was all right in the matter, and
he did not mean to make the innocent suffer for the
guilty.

" Now let us go to bed, Tony," he said in a friendly manner.   "You don't want to go with him, do
you?"

" No," said Tony. " I never want to see him
again."

"I shouldn't think you would. He's a rascal and a thief."

"I hope you don't think I wanted to rob the house," said Tony.

"No; I don't believe you're a bit like him; what makes you go with him?"

"I won't any more."

"He isn't your father?"

"No; I don't know who my father is."

"That's strange," said Abner, who had seen but little of the world. Every one that he knew had a a father, and knew who that father was. He could not realize that any one could have an experience like Tony's.

"I wish I did know my father," said Tony, thoughtfully. "I'm alone in the world now."

"What do you mean to do?"

"I'll go off by myself to-morrow, away from Rudolph. I never want to see him again."

"Have you got any money?"

They had now got back into the chamber, and were taking off their clothes.

"I've got five cents," answered Tony.

"Is that all?"

"Yes; but I don't mind; I'll get along some-how."

Tony had always got along somehow. He had never—at least not for long at a time—known what it was to have a settled home or a permanent shelter. Whether the world owed him a living or not, he had always got one, such as it was, and though he had often been cold and hungry, here he was at fourteen; well and strong, and with plenty of pluck and courage to carry with him into the life struggle that was opening before him. Abner's training had been different, and he wondered at the coolness with which Tony contemplated the future. But he was too sleepy to wonder long at anything, and with a yawn he lapsed into slumber.

Tony did not go to sleep immediately. He had need to be thoughtful. He had made up his mind to be his own master henceforth, but Rudolph, he knew, would have a word to say on that point. In getting away the next morning he must manage to give the tramp a wide berth. It would be better for him to go to some distant place, where, free from interference, he could make his own living.

There was another thought that came to him. Somewhere in the world he might come across a father or mother, or more distant relative—one of whom he would not be ashamed, as he was of the companion who tried to draw him into crime. This was the last thought in his mind, as he sank into a sound sleep from which he did not awaken till he was called to breakfast.

CHAPTER VI.

ABNER'S RUSE.

To say that Rudolph was angry when he recovered from the temporary insensibility occasioned by his fall, would be a very mild expression. He had not only been thwarted in his designs, but suffered violence and humiliation in presence of the boy of whom he regarded himself as the guardian. He thirsted for revenge, if not on Abner, then on Tony, whom it would be safer to maltreat and abuse.

Anger is unreasonable, and poor Tony would have fared badly, if he had fallen into Rudolph's clutches just then. It made no difference that Abner had exonerated Tony from any share in the unpleasant surprise he had met. He determined to give him a severe beating, nevertheless.

There is an old proverb: "You must catch your hare before you cook it." This did not occur to the tramp. He never supposed Tony would have the hardihood or courage to give him the slip.

The remainder of the night spent by Tony in sleeping was less pleasantly spent by Rudolph in the barn.

He meant to be up early, as he knew he was liable to arrest on account of his last night's attempt, and lie in wait for Tony, who, he supposed, would wait for breakfast.

He was right there.   Tony did remain for breakfast.   The farmer—Mr. Coleman—had already been
informed of Rudolph's attempted burglary, and he
did Tony the justice to exonerate him from any
share in it.

" What are you going to do, my boy? " he asked
at the breakfast table.

" I am going to set up for myself," answered
Tony, cheerfully.

" That's right.   Have nothing more to do with
that man.   He can only do you harm.   Have you
got any money? "

" I've got five cents."

" That isn't enough to buy a farm."

" Not a very large one," said Tony, smiling.

Abner nearly choked with laughter.   This was a
joke which he could appreciate.

" I don't think I'll go to farming," continued
Tony.

" You can stay here a week or two," said the
farmer, hospitably, " till you get time to look
round."

" Thank you," said Tony.   " You are very kind,
but I don't think it will be safe.   Rudolph will be on
the watch for me."

" The man you came with? "

" Yes."

" Guess he won't touch you while I'm round,"
said Abner.

" I don't think he'll want to tackle you again,"
said Tony.

"Didn't I lay him out though?" said Abner, with a grin. "He thought it was you, ho! ho!"

"He didn't think so long," said Tony. I haven't got such an arm as you."

Abner was pleased with this compliment to his prowess, and wouldn't have minded another tussle with the tramp.

"Where do you think that chap you call Rudolph is?" he asked.

"He's searching for me, I expect," said Tony. "If I'm not careful he'll get hold of me."

Just then a neighbor's boy, named Joe, came to the house on an errand. He was almost Tony's size. He waited about, not seeming in any hurry to be gone.

"Abner," said the farmer, "if you've got nothing else to do, you may load up the wagon with hay, and carry it to Castleton. We shall have more than we want."

"All right," said Abner.

"May I go, too?" May I ride on the hay?" asked Joe, eagerly.

"Will your father let you?" asked the farmer.

"Oh, yes; he won't mind."

"Then you may go," was the reply. "Do you want to go, too, Tony?"

Tony was about to say yes, when an idea seized him.

"If the other boy goes, Rudolph will think it is I, and he will follow the wagon. That will give me a chance of getting off in another direction."

"So it will," said Abner. "What a head-piece you've got," he added, admiringly. "I wouldn't have thought of that."

Abner's head-piece was nothing to boast of. He had strength of body, but to equalize matters his mind was not equally endowed.

The plan was disclosed to Joe, who willingly agreed to enter into it. This was the more feasible because he was of about Tony's size, and wore a hat just like his.

The hay was loaded, and the wagon started off with Abner walking alongside. Joe was perched on top, nearly buried in the hay, but with his hat rising from the mass. This was about all that could be seen of him.

They had gone about half a mile when from the bushes by the roadside Rudolph emerged. He had seen the hat, and felt sure that Tony was trying to escape him in this way.

"Well," said Abner, with a grin, as he recognized his midnight foe, "how do you feel this morning?"

"None the better for you, curse you!" returned the tramp, roughly.

Abner laughed.

"That's what I thought," he said, cracking his whip.

Rudolph would like to have punished him then and there for his humiliation of the night before, but Abner looked too powerful as he strode along manfully with vigorous steps. Besides, he had a heavy whip in his hand, which the tramp suspected would be used unhesitatingly if there were occasion. The prospect was not inviting. But, at any rate, Rudolph could demand that Tony be remitted to his custody.

"Where's my boy?" asked the tramp, keeping at a safe distance.

"Didn't know you had a boy," said Abner.

"I mean that villain Tony. Is that he on the load of hay?"

"Kinder looks like him," answered Abner, grinning.

Rudolph looked up and caught sight of the hat.

"Come down here, Tony," he said sternly.

Joe, who had been instructed what to do, answered not a word.

"Come down here, if you know what's best for you," continued the tramp.

"Guess he's hard of hearing," laughed Abner.

"Stop your wagon," said Rudolph, furiously; "I want to get hold of him."

"Couldn't do it," said Abner, coolly. "I'm in a hurry."

"Will you give me the boy or not?" demanded the tramp, hoarsely.

"He can get off and go along with you if he wants to," said Abner. "Do you want to get down, Tony?"

"No!" answered the supposed Tony.

"You see, squire, he prefers to ride," said Abner. "Can't blame him much. I'd do it in his place."

"Where are you going?" demanded the tramp,

who hadn't discovered that the voice was not that
of Tony.

"I'm going to Castleton," answered Abner.

"Are you going to leave the hay there?"

"Yes, that's what I calc'late to do."

"How far is it?"

"Six miles."

"I'll walk along, too."

"Better not, squire, you'll get tired."

"I'll risk that."

Of course Rudolph's plan was manifest. When
the hay was unloaded, of course Tony would have
to get down. Then he would get hold of him.

"You can do just as you've a mind to," said
Abner. "You'll be company to Tony and me, but
you needn't put yourself out on our account, hey,
Tony?"

There was a smothered laugh on top of the hay,
which the tramp heard. His eyes snapped viciously,
and he privately determined to give Tony a settle-
ment in full for all his offenses just as soon as he
got hold of him."

So they jogged on, mile after mile. Abner walked
on one side, swinging his whip, and occasionally
cracking it. The tramp walked on the other side
of the road, and the boy rode along luxuriously em-
bedded in his fragrant couch of hay. Abner from
time to time kept up the tramp's illusions by calling
out, "Tony, you must take keer, or you'll fall off."

"I'll catch him if he does," said Rudolph, grimly.

"So you will," chuckled Abner. "You'd like to, wouldn't you?"

"Certainly. He is my son," said Rudolph.

"Do you hear that, Tony? He says you're his son," said Abner, grinning again.

There was another laugh from the boy on the load of hay.

"You won't find anything to laugh at when I get hold of you," muttered Rudolph.

So they rode into Castleton.

From time to time Abner, as he thought how neatly the tramp had been sold, burst into a loud laugh, which was echoed from the hay wagon. Rudolph was not only angry, but puzzled.

"Does the boy hope to escape me?" he asked himself. "If so, he will find himself badly mistaken. He will find that I am not to be trifled with."

"Say, squire, what makes you look so glum?" asked Abner. "Maybe it's because I didn't let you in when you called so late last night. We don't receive visitors after midnight."

Rudolph scowled, but said nothing.

"How long has the boy been with you?" asked Abner, further.

"Since he was born," answered the tramp. "Ain't I his father?"

"I don't know. If it's a conundrum I give it up."

"Well, I am, and no one has a right to keep him from me," said the tramp, in a surly manner.

"I wouldn't keep him from you for a minute," said Abner, innocently.

"You are doing it now."

"No, I ain't."

"I can't get at him on that hay."

"He can come down if he wants to. I don't stop him. You can come down if you want to, Tony," he said, looking up to where the boy's hat was visible.

Tony did not answer, and Abner continued:

"You see he don't want to come. He'd rather ride. You know he's been sick," said Abner, with a grin, "and he's too delicate to walk. He ain't tough, like you and me."

"He'll need to be tough," muttered the tramp, as he thought of the flogging he intended to give Tony.

"What did you say?"

"Never mind."

"Oh, I don't mind," said Abner. "You can say what you want to. This is a free country, only you can't do what you've a mind to."

Rudolph wished that he had a double stock of strength. It was very provoking to be laughed at and derided by Abner without being able to revenge himself. A pistol or a knife would make him even with the countryman, but Rudolph was too much of a coward to commit such serious crimes when there was so much danger of detection and punishment.

At last they entered Castleton.

The hay was to be delivered to a speculator, who

collected large quantities of it, and forwarded over the railroad to a large city.

It had to be weighed, and Abner drove at once to the hay scales.

"Now," thought Rudolph, with exultation, "the boy must come down, and I shall get hold of him."

"I guess you'd better slide down," said Abner. "I can't sell you for hay, Tony."

There was a movement, and then the boy slid down, Abner catching him as he descended.

Rudolph's face changed ominously when he saw that it wasn't Tony who made his appearance.

"What does this mean?" he demanded furiously.

"What's the matter?"

"This isn't Tony."

"Come to look at him, it isn't," said Abner, with a twinkle in his eye.

"Didn't you say it was Tony?" asked the tramp, exasperated.

"I guess I was mistaken, squire," said Abner, grinning.

"Where is he?"

"I don't know, I'm sure. It seems he didn't come. Guess he must have given us the slip."

The tramp, unable to control his rage, burst into a volley of execrations.

"Hope you feel better, squire," said Abner, when he got through.

The tramp strode off, vowing dire vengeance against both Abner and Tony.

" What does this mean ?" demanded the tramp furiously   " This isn't
Tony."—(See page 45.)

CHAPTER VII.

A STRANGE HOTEL.

From the upper window in the farm house, which was situated on elevated ground, Tony saw his old guardian follow Abner. Thus the way was opened for his escape. He waited, however, a short time to make sure that all was safe, and then bade farewell to the farmer and his wife, thanking them heartily for their kindness to him."

"Won't you stay longer with us?" asked the farmer. "You can as well as not."

"Thank you," answered Tony, "but I wouldn't dare to. Rudolph may be back for me, and I want to get away before he has a chance."

"Are you going to walk?" asked the farmer's wife.

"Yes," said Tony. "I've only got five cents in my pocket, and I can't ride far on that."

"I'm afraid you will be tired," said she, sympathetically.

"Oh, I'm used to tramping," returned Tony, lightly. "I don't mind that at all."

"Can't you put up some dinner for him, wife?" suggested the farmer. "It'll make him hungry, walking."

"To be sure I will," she replied, and a large supply of eatables were put in a paper, sufficient to last Tony twenty-four hours, at least.

The farmer deliberated whether he should not of·
fer our hero half a dollar besides, but he was naturally close, so far as money was concerned, and he
decided in the negative.

So Tony set out, taking a course directly opposite
to that pursued by Abner.   In this way he thought
he should best avoid the chance of meeting Rudolph.

He walked easily, not being in any special hurry,
and whenever he felt at all tired he stopped by the
wayside to rest.   Early in the afternoon he lay
down under a tree in the pasture and fell asleep.
He was roused by a cold sensation, and found that
a dog had pressed his cold nose against his cheek.

"Haven't you any more manners, sir?" demanded
Tony, good-naturedly.

The dog wagged his tail, and looked friendly.

"It's a hint that I must be on my journey," he
thought.

About five o'clock he felt that it was about time
to look out for a night's rest.   A hotel was, of
course, out of the question, and he looked about for
a farm house.   The nearest dwelling was a small
one, of four rooms, setting back from the road,
down a lane.

"Perhaps I can get in there," thought Tony.

An old man, with a patriarchal beard, whose neglected and squalid dress seemed to indicate poverty,
was sitting on the door-step.

"Good evening." said Tony.

"Who are you?" demanded the old man, suspiciously.

"I am a poor traveler," said Tony.

"A tramp!" said the old man, in the same suspicious tone.

"Yes, I suppose so," said Tony, although he did not like the title overmuch.

"Well, I've got nothing for you," said the old man, roughly.

"I don't want anything except the chance to sleep."

"Don't you want any supper?"

"No, I've got my supper here," returned our hero, producing his paper of provisions.

"What have you got there?" asked the old man, with an eager look.

"Some bread and butter and cold meat."

"It looks good," said the other, with what Tony thought to be a longing look.

"I'll share it with you, if you'll let me sleep here to-night," said Tony.

"Will you?" the other answered.

"Yes; there's enough for both of us."

The old man was a miser, as Tony suspected. He was able to live comfortably, but he deprived himself of the necessaries of life in order to hoard away money. His face revealed that to Tony. He had nearly starved himself, but he had not overcome his natural appetites, and the sight of Tony's supper gave him a craving for it.

"I don't know," he said, doubtfully. "If I let you sleep here you might get up in the night and rob me."

Tony laughed.

"You don't look as if you had anything worth stealing," he said, candidly.

"You're right, quite right," said old Ben Hayden, for this was his name. "I've only saved a little money—a very little—to pay my funeral expenses. You wouldn't want to take that?"

"Oh, no," said Tony. "I wouldn't take it if you'd give it to me."

"You wouldn't? why not?"

"Because you need it yourself. If you were a rich man it would be different."

"So it would," said old Hayden. "You're a good boy—an excellent boy. I'll trust you. You can stay."

"Then let us eat supper," said Tony.

He sat down on the door-step, and gave the old man half of his supply of food. He was interested to see the avidity with which he ate it.

"Is it good?" he asked.

"I haven't eaten anything so good for a long time. I couldn't afford to buy food."

"I am sorry for you."

"You haven't got any left for breakfast," said the old man.

"Oh, somebody will give me breakfast," said Tony. "I always get taken care of somehow."

"You are young and strong."

"Yes."

"Do you travel around all the time?"

"Yes; but I hope to get a chance to go to work soon; I'd rather live in one place."

"You might live with me if I were not so poor," said the old man.

"Thank you," answered Tony, politely; but it did not appear to him that it was exactly such a home as he would choose.

"Do you live alone?" he asked.

"Yes."

"I didn't know but you might be married."

"I was married when I was a young man, but my wife died long ago."

"Why don't you marry again?" inquired Tony, half in fun.

"I couldn't afford it," answered Hayden, frightened at the suggestion. "Women have terrible appetites."

"Have they?" returned Tony, amused.

"And I can't get enough for myself to eat."

"Have you always lived here?"

"No; I lived in England when I was a young man."

"What made you leave it?"

"Why do you ask me that?" demanded old Ben, suspiciously.

"Oh, if it's a secret, don't tell me," said Tony, indifferently.

"Who said it was a secret?" said the old man, irritably.

"Nobody that I know of."

"Then why do you ask me such questions?"

The old man surveyed Tony with a look of doubt, as if he thought the boy were laying a trap for him.

"Don't answer anything you don't want to," said our hero. "I only asked for the sake of saying something."

"I don't mind telling, said old Ben, more calmly. "It was because I was so poor. I thought I could do better in America."

"And didn't you?"

"When I was able to work. Now I'm weak and poor, and can't always get enough to eat."

"Do you own this place?"

"Yes, but it's a very poor place. It isn't worth much."

"I shouldn't think it was," said Tony.

"You're a good lad—an excellent lad. You see how poor I am."

"Of course I do, and I'm sorry for you. I would help you, only I am very poor myself."

"Have you got any money?" asked Ben, with interest.

"I've got five cents," answered Tony, laughing. I hope you've got more than that."

"A little more—a very little more," said Ben, cautiously.

The old miser began to consider whether he couldn't charge Tony five cents for his lodging, but sighed at the recollection that Tony had already paid for it in advance by giving him a supper.

When eight o'clock came the miser suggested going to bed.

"I haven't any lights," he said; "candles cost so much. Besides, a body's better off in bed."

"I'm willing to go to bed," said Tony. "I've walked a good deal to-day, and I'm tired."

They went into the house. There was a heap of rags in the corner of the room when they entered.

"That's my bed," said old Ben; "it all I have."

"I can sleep on the floor," said Tony.

He took off his jacket, and rolled it up for a pillow, and stretched himself out on the bare floor. He had often slept so before.

CHAPTER VIII.

TONY HIRES OUT AS A COOK AND HOUSEKEEPER.

Tony was not slow in going to sleep. Neither his hard bed nor his strange bed-chamber troubled him. He could sleep anywhere. That was one of the advantages of his checkered life.

Generally he slept all night without awaking, but to-night, for some unknown reason, he awoke about two o'clock. It was unusually light for that hour, and so he was enabled to see what at first startled him. The old man was out of bed, and on his knees in the center of the room. He had raised a plank, forming a part of the flooring, and had raised from beneath it a canvass bag full of gold pieces. He was taking them out and counting them, apparently quite unconscious of Tony's presence.

Tony raised himself on his elbow, and looked at him. It occurred to him that for a man so suspicious it was strange that he should expose his hoard before a stranger. Something, however, in the old man's look led him to think that he was in a sleep-walking fit.

"Ninety-five, ninety-six, ninety-seven," Tony heard him count; "that makes nine hundred and seventy dollars, all gold, good, beautiful gold. Nobody knows the old man is so rich. There's another bag, too. There are one hundred pieces in that. Three more, and this will be full, too. Nobody must know, nobody must know."

He put back the pieces, replaced the bag in its hiding-place, and then putting back the plank, laid down once more on his heap of rags.

"How uneasy he would be," thought Tony, "if he knew I had seen his treasures. But I wouldn't rob him for the world, although the money would do me good, and he makes no use of it except to look at it."

If Tony was honest, it was an instinctive feeling. It could not have been expected of one reared as he had been. But, singular as it may seem, beyond a vague longing, he felt no temptation to deprive old Ben of his money.

"Let him get what satisfaction he can from it," he said to himself. "I hope he'll keep it till he dies. I am only afraid that some night some one will see him counting the gold who will want to take it."

Tony went to bed again, and slept till six. Then he was awakened by a piteous groaning, which he soon found proceeded from the other bed.

"What's the matter?" he asked.

"Who's there?" demanded Ben, terrified.

"It's only I. Don't you remember you let me sleep here last night?"

"O, yes; I remember now. I'm sick; very sick."

"How do you feel?"

"I'm aching and trembling all over. Do you

think I am going to die?" he asked, with a startled look.

"Oh, no, I guess not," said Tony, reassuringly. "Everybody is sick now and then."

"I never felt so before," groaned Ben. "I'm an old man. Don't you think—don't you really think I shall die?"

He looked appealingly at Tony, as if the fiat of life and death lay with him.

Tony, of course, knew nothing of medicine or of diseases, but he had the sense to understand that the old man would be more likely to recover if his terror could be allayed, and he said, lightly:

"Oh, it's only a trifle. You've taken cold, very likely. A cup of hot tea would be good for you."

"I haven't any tea," groaned Ben. "It costs a great deal, and I'm very poor. I can't afford to buy it."

Tony smiled to himself, remembering the hoard of gold under the floor, but he would not refer to it, at least not at present.

"Are you sure you haven't got a little money?" he asked. "If you want to get well, you must be made comfortable."

"It's hard to be poor," whined Ben.

"I guess you've got some money," said Tony. "You'd better let me go to the store, and buy some tea and a fresh roll for you."

"How much will it cost?" asked Ben.

"I can get some bread, and tea, and sugar for thirty or forty cents," answered Tony.

"Forty cents! It's frightful!" exclaimed Ben. "I—I guess I'll do without it."

"Oh, well, if you prefer to lie there and die its none of my business," said Tony, rather provoked at the old man's perverse folly.

"But I don't want to die," whined Ben.

"Then do as I tell you."

Tony jumped out of bed, unrolled his coat, and put it on.

"Now," said he, "I'm ready to go for you, if you'll give me the money."

"But you may take it, and not come back," said the old man, suspiciously.

"If you think you can't trust me, you needn't," said Tony. "I've offered to do you a favor."

"I think I'll go myself," said Ben.

He tried to raise himself, but a twinge of pain compelled him to lie down again."

"No, I can't," he said.

"Well, do you want me to go for you?"

"Yes," answered Ben, reluctantly.

"Then give me the money."

Still more reluctantly Ben produced twenty-five cents from his pocket.

"Isn't that enough?" he asked.

"Better give me more," said Tony.

He produced ten cents more, and vowed it was all the money he had in the world.

Tony decided not to contradict his assertion, but to make this go as far as it would. He put on his hat and started out. He meant also to call at the doctor's, and asked him to call round, for he thought it possible that the old man might be seriously sick.

First, however, he went to the grocery store, which had only just been opened, and obtained the articles which he had mentioned to Ben as likely to do him good.

Next he called at the house of the village doctor, obtaining the direction from the storekeeper. In a few words he made known his errand.

"Old Ben sick!" said Doctor Compton. "What's the matter with him?"

Tony explained how he appeared to be affected.

"How did you happen to be in his house?" asked the doctor, with curiosity. "You are not a relation of his, are you?"

Tony laughed.

"I don't think he would let me into the house if I were," he said. "He would be suspicious of me."

"Then how does it happen that you were with him?"

Tony explained.

"He has been repaid for taking you in," said the doctor. "I'll put on my hat, and go right over with you."

After Tony left the house, old Ben lay and tormented himself with the thought that the boy would never come back. "Just as like as not," he thought, "he will go off with the money, and leave me here to die."

Then he tried to sit up, but without success.

Half an hour later he was relieved by seeing the door open, and Tony enter. But he looked dismayed when he saw the doctor.

"What did you come for?" he asked, peevishly.

"To see what I can do for you, Mr. Hayden. Let me feel your pulse."

"But I can't afford to have a doctor. I am poor, and can't pay you," whined old Ben.

"We'll talk about that afterward."

"You can't charge when I didn't send for you."

"Make your mind easy. I won't charge for this visit. Let me feel your pulse."

Old Ben no longer opposed medical treatment, finding it would cost nothing.

"Am I going to die?" he asked, with an anxious look.

"You need nourishing food and care, that is all," was the reply. "You have had a chill, and you are reduced by insufficient food."

"I have some bread and tea here," said Tony.

"Do you know how to make the tea?" asked the doctor.

"Yes," said Tony.

"Then make a fire, and boil it at once. And, by the way, Mr. Hayden needs somebody to be with him for a few days. Can you stay with him and look after him?"

"If he will give me money enough to buy what he needs," said Tony.

"Will you do it, Mr. Hayden?" asked the doctor.

Old Ben whined that he was poor, and had no money, but the doctor interrupted him impatiently.

"That's all nonsense," he said. "You may not have much money, but you've got some, and you'll die if you don't spend some on yourself. If you don't agree to it, I shall advise this boy here to leave you to your fate. Then your only resource will be to go to the poor-house."

This proposal was not acceptable to Ben, who was unwilling to leave the house where his treasures were concealed. He therefore reluctantly acceded to the doctor's conditions, and Tony got his breakfast. Despite his sickness, he relished the tea and toast, and for the moment forgot what it cost.

"Well," thought Tony to himself with a smile, "I've got a situation as plain cook and housekeeper. I wonder how long it will last, and what'll come of it. I don't believe Rudolph will look for me here."

But in this Tony was mistaken.

CHAPTER IX.

THE FACE AT THE WINDOW.

Tony was not only cook and housekeeper, but he was sick-nurse as well. Nor were his duties easy. The main difficulty was about getting money to buy what was absolutely necessary. This was very aggravating, especially since Tony knew what he did about Ben's hidden treasure. Moreover, he had reason to suspect that Ben had more money concealed elsewhere.

One morning Tony went to Ben for money, saying:

"There isn't a scrap of food in the house, except a little tea."

"You can make some tea. That will do," said Ben.

"It may do for you, but it won't for me," said Tony, resolutely. "I ain't going to stay here to starve."

"It costs a sight to support two people," whined the old man.

"I don't know about that. I've only spent two dollars in six days. You don't call that much, do you?"

"Two dollars!" ejaculated the old man, terrified. "O, it's too much. I am ruined!"

"Are you?" said Tony, coolly. "Then all I can say is, you're easy ruined. I want half a dollar."

"I shan't give it to you," snarled Ben.

"Do you mean to starve?"

"I won't part with all I have. You are robbing me."

"That won't make much difference, as you'll be dead in three days," said Tony.

"What?" almost shrieked Ben, in dismay. "Who told you so? The doctor?"

"No."

"You ain't goin' to murder me, are you?"

"No; you are going to murder yourself."

"What do you mean?" demanded Ben, peevishly.

"You're not willing to buy anything to eat," explained Tony, "and you can't live above three days on nothing."

"Is that all? What made you frighten me so?" complained Ben, angrily.

"I only told you the truth. Are you going to give me the money?"

"Perhaps you'll tell me where I am to get so much money?" said Ben, in the same tone.

"I will tell you if you want me to," answered Tony.

"Where?" asked Ben, eagerly.

"Under the floor," returned Tony, composedly.

"What!" screamed Ben, in consternation.

"Just where I said. There's plenty of money under that plank."

"Who told you?" groaned the old man, livid with terror. "Have—have you taken any?"

"Not a dollar. It's all there. You needn't be frightened."

"Have you been spying when I was asleep?" demanded Ben, incensed.

"No, I haven't. That ain't my style," answered Tony, independently.

"You did. I know you did."

"Then you know too much."

"How could you find out, then?"

"If you want to know, I'll tell you. The first night I was here you got up in your sleep and took up the board. Then you drew out two bags of gold pieces and counted them."

"Oh, I'm ruined! I'm undone!" lamented Ben, when he found that his secret had been discovered.

"I don't see how you are."

"I shall be robbed. There's only a little there— only a few dollars to bury me."

"I guess you mean to have a tall funeral, then," said Tony, coolly. "There's as much as a thousand dollars there."

"No, no—only fifty," answered the old man.

"There's no use talking, I know better. If you don't believe it, suppose I take up the bags and count the pieces."

"No, no!"

"Just as you say. All is, you've got plenty of money, and I know it, and if you ain't willing to use some of it, I'll go off and leave you alone."

"Don't go," said Ben, hastily. "You're a good boy. You wouldn't rob a poor old man, would you?"

"Nor a rich old man either; but I don't mean to

starve. So give me fifty cents, and I'll go over to
the store and get some fresh bread and butter, and
tea and sugar."

"No matter about the butter. It costs too much."

"I want butter myself. My constitution requires
it," said Tony. You needn't eat it if you don't
want to."

Ben groaned again, but he produced the money
required, and Tony soon returned from the grocery
store with small supplies of the articles he had
named.

"Now we'll have some breakfast," said Tony,
cheerfully. "Don't you feel hungry?"

"A—a little," acknowledged Ben, reluctantly.
"I wish I wasn't. It costs so much to live."

"I don't think it costs you much," said Tony.
"This morning I'm going to give you a boiled egg
besides your tea and toast."

"Where did you get it?"

"I bought it at the store."

"I can't afford it," groaned the old man.

"You may as well eat it as it's here. I bought
two, one for myself."

"How much did you pay?"

"Three cents for two."

Ben groaned again, but when breakfast was ready
he showed an unusually good appetite, and did not
refrain from partaking of the egg, expensive as it
was.

Dr. Compton came in the next morning, and pro-
nounced the old man better and stronger.

"Shall I be able to get up soon, doctor?" asked Ben.

"In a day or two, I think."

Ben heaved a sigh of relief.

"I'm glad of it," he said. "I can't afford to be sick."

"Has it cost you much?" asked the doctor, amused.

"It costs a sight to live. He eats a good deal," indicating Tony.

"He's a growing boy; but he's worth all he costs you. You'd better ask him to stay with you a few weeks, till your strength is entirely recovered."

"No, no; I can't afford it," said Ben, hastily. "He's a good boy; but he's very hearty—very hearty."

Tony laughed.

"Don't vex him, doctor," said our hero. "I'm tired of staying here. I want to get out on the road again. There isn't much fun in staying shut up here."

Ben looked relieved. He had feared that Tony would be reluctant to go.

"Right, boy," he said, "you're right. It's a dull place. You'll be better off to go."

"You have been lucky to have him here during your sickness," said the doctor. "Without his care, or that of some one else, you would probably have died."

"But I won't die now?" asked old Ben, anxiously, peering up into the doctor's face.

"Not at present, I hope.   But you must live better than you have been accustomed to do or you
will fall sick again."

"I shall be glad to get away," said Tony, hurriedly, to the doctor, outside of the house.   "I'm used
to tramping, and I can't stand it much longer.
There's one thing I want to tell you before I go, and
I might as well do it now."

"Go on, my boy."

"I'm afraid the old man will be robbed some
time."

"Is there anything to steal?"

"Yes; I think I had better tell you about it."

Tony, in a low tone, imparted to Dr. Compton the
discovery he had made of the old miser's hoards.

"I suspected as much," said the doctor.   "I will
do what I can to induce Ben to have the gold moved
to a place of safety, but I don't feel confident of my
ability to do it.   Such men generally like to have
their hoards within their own reach."

*   *   *   *   *   *

Two nights later, Tony woke shortly after midnight.   It was a bright, moonlight night, as on the
first night he slept there.   Again he saw Ben
crouched on the floor, with the plank removed from
its place, engaged in counting his hoards.   The old
man had recovered enough strength to get out of
bed without assistance.   This time, too, he was
broad awake.

Tony was not the only witness of the spectacle.
Casting his eyes toward the window he was startled

by seeing a dark, sinister face, pressed against the pane, almost devouring the old man and his gold.

It was a face he well knew, and he trembled not alone for Ben, but for himself.

It was the face of Rudolph, the tramp.

CHAPTER X.

THE TRAMPS UNEXPECTED DEFEAT.

"Has Rudolph tracked me, or is it only accident that has brought him here?"

This was the thought which naturally suggested itself to our hero, as in a very disturbed state of mind he stared at Rudolph through the uncertain light.

He decided that it was accident, for as yet the tramp did not appear to have discovered him. His eyes were fastened upon old Ben with unmistakable cupidity. It was the gold that attracted him, and between him and the possession of the gold it seemed as if there were no obstacle to intervene. What was the old man's feeble strength, more feeble still through disease, against this powerful man?

Tony felt the difficulties of the position. Not only would the gold be taken, but as soon as Rudolph discovered him, as he would, he too would fall into the power of the tramp.

Old Ben had not yet discovered the sinister face at the window. He was too busily occupied with his pleasant employment of counting over his gold for the hundredth time, it might be, to be aware of the dangerous witness at the window.

But he was speedily aroused by the noise of the window being raised from the outside.

Then he turned with a startled look which quickly deepened into astonishment and dismay as he caught the lowering look fixed upon him. There was more than this. There was recognition besides.

"You here?" he gasped, mechanically gathering up the gold in his trembling fingers, with the intention of replacing it in the bag.

"Yes, Ben, it's me," answered the tramp, with a sneer. "May I come in?"

"No, no!" ejaculated the old man, hastily.

"I think I must," returned the tramp, in the same mocking tone. "I came to see you as an old friend, but I never dreamed you were so rich. That's a pretty lot of gold you have there."

"Rich!" repeated Ben, with his usual whine. "I'm very poor."

"That looks like it."

"It's only a few dollars—enough to bury me."

"Very well, Ben, I'll take charge of it, and when you need burial I'll attend to it. That's fair, isn't it?"

Rudolph, who had paused outside, now raised the window to its full height, and despite the old man's terrified exclamations, bounded lightly into the room.

"Help! help! thieves!" screamed Ben, almost beside himself with terror, as he spread his feeble hands over the gold which he had so imprudently exposed.

"Hold your jaw, you driveling old idiot?" said Rudolph, harshly, "or I'll give you something to yell about."

"Help, Tony, help!" continued the old man.

The tramp's eyes, following the direction of Ben's, discovered our hero on his rude bed in the corner of the room. A quick gleam of exultation shot from them as he made this discovery.

"Ho, ho!" he laughed with a mirth that boded ill to Tony, "so I've found you at last, have I? You served me a nice trick the other day, didn't you? I owe you something for that."

"I hoped I should never set eyes on you again," said Tony.

"I've no doubt you did. You undertook to run away from me, did you? I knew I should come across you sooner or later."

While this conversation was going on, Ben glanced from one to the other in surprise, his attention momentarily drawn away from his own troubles.

"Do you know this boy, Rudolph?" he inquired.

"I should think I did," answered the tramp, grimly. "You can ask him."

"*Who is he?*" asked Ben, evidently excited.

"What is that to you?" returned Rudolph. "It's a boy I picked up, and have taken care of, and this is his gratitude to me, and I've had a long chase to find him."

"Is this true?" asked Ben, turning to Tony.

"Some of it is true," said our hero. "I've been with him ever since I could remember, and I ran away because he wanted me to join him in robbing a house. He calls me his son sometimes, but I know he is not my father."

"How do you know?" demanded the tramp sternly.

"Didn't you say so just now?"

"It was none of the old man's business, and I did not care what I told him."

"There's something within me tells me that there's no relationship between us," said Tony, boldly.

"Is there, indeed," sneered the tramp. "Is there anything within you tells you you are going to get a good flogging?"

"No, there isn't."

"Then you needn't trust it, for that is just what is going to happen."

He advanced toward Tony in a threatening manner, when he was diverted from his purpose by seeing the old man hastily gathering up the gold with the intention of putting it away. Punishment could wait, he thought, but the gold must be secured now.

"Not so fast, Ben!" he said. "You must lend me some of that."

"I can't," said Ben, hurrying all the faster. "It's all I have, and I am very poor."

"I am poorer still, for I haven't a red to bless myself with. Come, I won't take all, but some I must have."

He stooped over, and began to grasp at the gold pieces, some of which were heaped up in piles upon the floor.

Even the weakest are capable of harm when ex-

asperated, and Ben, feeble as he was, was gifted
with supernatural strength when he saw himself
likely to lose the hoards of a lifetime, and his anger
rose to fever heat against the scoundrel whom he
had known years before to be utterly unprincipled.

With a cry like that of a wild beast he sprang
upon the tramp, who, in his crouching position,
was unable to defend himself against a sudden attack. Rudolph fell with violence backward, striking his head with great force against the brick
hearth. Strong as he was, it was too much for him,
and he lay stunned and insensible, with the blood
gushing from a wound in his head.

The old man stood appalled at the consequence of
his sudden attack.

"Have I killed him? Shall I be hanged?" he
asked, with anguish.

"No, he's only stunned!" said Tony, springing
over the floor with all his wits about him. "We
have no time to lose."

"To run away? I can't leave my gold," said Ben.

"I don't mean that. We must secure him against
doing us any harm when he recovers. Have you
got some stout cord?"

"Yes, yes," said Ben, beginning to understand
our hero's design. "Stay, I'll get it right away."

"You'd better, for he may come to any minute."

The old man fumbled round until in some out-of-
the-way corner, where he had laid away a store of
odds and ends, he discovered a quantity of stout
cord.

"Will that do?" he asked.

"Just the thing," said Tony.

The boy set to work with rapid hands to tie the prostrate tramp hand and foot. He was only afraid Rudolph would rouse to consciousness while the operation was going on, but the shock was too great, and he had sufficient time to do the job effectually and well.

"How brave you are," exclaimed the old man, admiringly. "I wouldn't dare to touch him."

"Nor I if he were awake. I didn't think you were so strong. He went over as if he were shot."

"Did he?" asked the old man, bewildered. "I don't know how I did it. I feel as weak as a baby now."

"It's lucky for us you threw yourself upon him as you did. A little more cord, Mr. Hayden. I want to tie him securely. You'd better be gathering up that gold, and putting it away before he comes to."

"So I will, so I will," said Ben, hastily.

Scarcely was the money put away in its place of concealment, when the tramp recovered from his fit of unconsciousness, and looked stupidly around him. Then he tried to move, and found himself hampered by his bonds. Looking up, he met the terrified gaze of old Ben, and the steady glance of Tony. Then the real state of the case flashed upon him, and he was filled with an overpowering rage at the audacity of his late charge, to whom he rightly attributed his present humiliating plight.

CHAPTER XI.

THE PRISONER.

" Let me up!" roared Rudolph, struggling vigorously with the cords that bound him.

Ben was terrified by his demonstration, and had half a mind to comply with his demand. But Tony had his wits about him, and felt that there was no safety in such a course.

"Don't you do it, Mr. Hayden!" he exclaimed, hastily.

"What! young jackanapes," said the tramp, scowling fiercely, " You dare to give him this advice?"

" Yes, I do," said Tony, boldly. " He will be a fool if he releases you."

" If he don't I'll kill him and you too," returned Rudolph.

" What shall I do?" added Ben, hopelessly.

He turned for advice to the boy, who was fifty years his junior. Strong and resolute spirits naturally assume the place of leading at any age.

"Do you know what he'll do if you untie him?" asked Tony.

" What will I do?" demanded Rudolph.

"You will steal this old man's money. It was what you were about to do when you fell over backwards."

"He threw me over," said the tramp, now gazing resentfully at Ben.

"I didn't mean to," said the terrified old man.

"You almost stunned me."

"I'm very sorry," stammered Ben.

"If you're very sorry, untie them cords and let me up."

"I didn't tie you."

"Who did?"

"The—the boy."

"You *dared* to do it?" exclaimed Rudolph, turning upon Tony with concentrated fury.

"Yes, I did," said Tony, calmly. "It was the only way to keep you out of mischief."

"Insolent puppy; if I only had my hands free I would strangle you both."

"You hear what he says?" said Tony, turning to old Ben. "Are you in favor of untying him now?"

"No, no!" exclaimed Ben, trembling. "He is a dreadful man. O, why did he come here?"

"I came for your gold, you fool, and I'll have it yet," said Rudolph, losing sight of all considerations of prudence.

"What shall I do?" asked the old man, wringing his hands in the excess of his terror.

"Let me up, and I won't hurt you," said the tramp, finding that he must control his anger for the present.

"Just now you said you would strangle the both of us, Rudolph."

" I'll strangle you, you cub, but I will do no harm
to the old man."

" You will take his gold."

" No."

" Don't you trust him, Mr. Hayden," said Tony.
' He will promise anything to get free, but he will
forget all about it when he is unbound."

" I'd like to choke you!" muttered Rudolph, who
meant thoroughly what he said.

" But what shall I do, Tony? I can't have him
in here all the time."

" I'll go and call for help to arrest him," said
Tony.

" And leave me alone with him?" asked Ben,
terrified.

" No; we will lock the door, and you shall go and
stay outside till I come back."

Tony's proposal was distasteful to Rudolph. He
had a wholesome dread of the law, and didn't fancy
the prospect of an arrest, especially as he knew that
the testimony of Tony and the old man would be
sufficient to insure him a prolonged term of imprisonment. He made a fresh and violent struggle
which portended danger to his captors.

" Come out quick," said Tony, hastily. " It is
not safe for you to stay here any longer."

The old man followed him nothing loth, and
Tony locked the door on the outside.

" Do you think he will get free?" asked Ben,
nervously.

" He may, and if he does there is no safety for
either of us till he is caught again.

"The door is locked."

"But he may get out of the window"

"Oh, my gold! my gold!" groaned Ben. "He may get it."

"Yes, he may; our only hope is to secure him as soon as possible."

"I am so weak I can't go fast. I am trembling in every limb."

"You must conceal yourself somewhere, and let me run on," said Tony, with decision. "There is no time to be lost."

"I don't know of any place."

"Here's a place. You will be safe here till I come for you."

Tony pointed to an old ruined shed, which they had just reached.

"Will you be sure and come for me."

"Yes; don't be alarmed. Only don't show yourself till you hear my voice."

Ben crept into the temporary shelter, glad that in his weakened condition he should not be obliged to go any farther. To be sure he tormented himself with the thought that even now the desperate tramp might be robbing him of his treasures. Still he had great confidence in what Tony had told him, and hope was mingled with his terror.

"He's a brave boy," he murmured. "I am glad he was with me, though he does eat a sight. Oh, how many wicked men there are in the world."

Tony hurried on to the village, where he lost no time in arousing a sufficient number to effect the capture of the burglar. He no longer felt any compunction in turning against his quondam guardian, recognizing him as his own enemy and the enemy of society.

"I owe him nothing," thought Tony. "What has he ever done for me? He is not my father. Probably he kidnapped me from my real home, and has made me an outcast and a tramp like himself. But I will be so no longer. I will learn a trade, or do something else to earn an honest livelihood. I mean to become a respectable member of society, if I can."

It took him half an hour before he could rouse the half-dozen men whom he considered necessary to effect the arrest and get them under way.

Meanwhile Rudolph was not idle.

It may be thought strange that he should have so much difficulty in freeing himself from the cords with which Tony had bound him. But it must be remembered that the boy had done his work well. The cord was stout and strong, and he had had time to tie it in many knots, so that even if one had been untied, the tramp would have found himself almost as far from liberty as ever.

After he had been locked in, Rudolph set about energetically to obtain release. He succeeded in raising himself to his feet, but as his ankles were tied together this did not do him much good. By main strength he tried to break the cords, but the only result was to chafe his wrists.

"What a fool I am," he exclaimed at length.

"The old man must have some table-knives about somewhere. With these I can cut the cords."

It was not till some time had elapsed, however, that this very obvious thought came to him. Further time was consumed in finding the knives. When found, they—there were two—proved so dull that even if he had had free use of one of his hands it would not have been found easy to make them of service. But when added to this was the embarrassment of his fettered hands, it will not excite surprise that it required a long time to sever the tough cords which bound him. But success came at length.

His arms were free, and he stretched them with exultation.

His ankles next demanded attention, but this was a much easier task.

"Now for revenge!" thought the tramp. "The boy shall rue this night's task, or my name is not Rudolph."

Whatever else he might do, he must secure the miser's gold. He had seen the hiding-place.

He removed the plank, and there, beneath him, visible in the moonlight, lay the much-coveted bags of golden treasure.

He rose from the floor, and, with the bags in his hand, jumped out of the still opened window.

But he was too late. Two strong men seized him, each by an arm, and said, sternly:

"You are our prisoner."

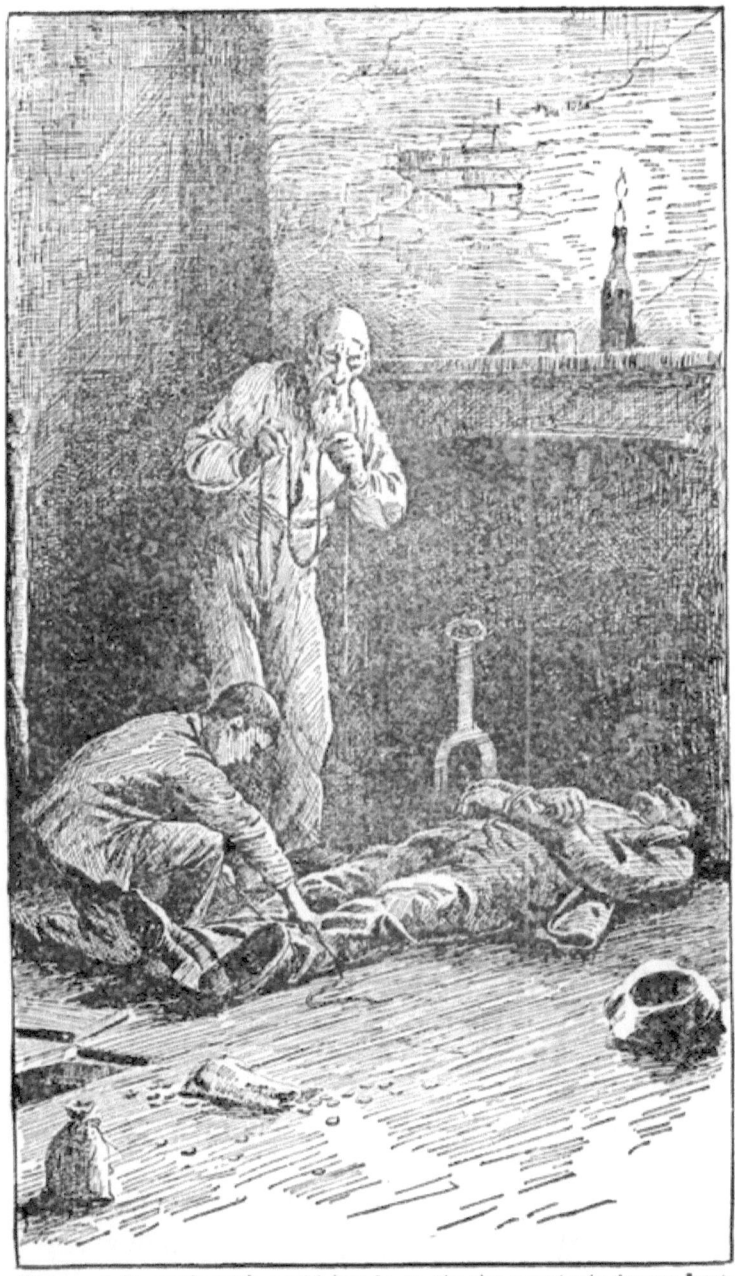

Tony set to work with rapid hands to tie the prostrate tramp hand and foot.—(See page 73.)

80

CHAPTER XII.

TONY STARTS OUT ONCE MORE.

It was not until after Rudolph's seizure that Ben, who had followed the extemporized police, discovered the bags of gold in the hands of the tramp.

"Give me my money!" he shrieked, in excitement and anguish. "Don't let him carry it off"

"It's safe, Ben," said one of the captors. "But who would have supposed you had so much money? '

"It isn't much," faltered the old man.

"The bags are pretty heavy," was the significant rejoinder. "Will you take two hundred dollars apiece for them?"

"No," said the old man, embarrassed.

"Then it seems there is considerable after all. But never mind. Take them, and take better care of them hereafter."

Ben advanced with as much alacrity as he could summon in his weakness, and stooped to pick up the bags. He had got hold of them when the tramp, whose feet were unconfined, aimed a kick at him which completely upset him.

Even though he fell, however, he did not lose his grip of the bags, but clung to them while crying with pain.

"Take that, you old fool!" muttered the tramp. "It's the first instalment of the debt I owe you."

"Take him away, take him away! He will murder me!" exclaimed old Ben, in terror.

"Come along. You've done mischief enough," said his captors, sternly, forcing the tramp along.

"I'll do more yet," muttered Rudolph.

He turned to Tony, who stood at a little distance watching the fate of his quondam companion.

"I've got a score to settle with you, young traitor. The day will come for that yet."

"I'm sorry for you, Rudolph." said Tony; "but you brought it on yourself."

"Bah! you hypocrite!" retorted the tramp. "I don't want any of your sorrow. It won't save you when the day of reckoning comes."

He was not allowed to say more, but was hurried away to the village lockup for detention until he could be conveyed to more permanent quarters.

Doctor Compton was among the party who had been summoned by Tony. He lingered behind, and took Ben apart.

"Mr. Hayden," he said, "I want to give you a piece of advice."

"What is it?" asked the old man.

"Don't keep this gold in your house. It isn't safe."

"Who do you think will take it?" asked Ben, with a scared look.

"None of those here this morning, unless this tramp should escape from custody."

"Do you think he will?" asked the old man, in terror.

"I think not; but he may."

"If he don't, what danger is there?"

"It will get about that you have money secreted here, and I venture to say it will be stolen before three months are over."

"It will kill me," said Ben, piteously.

"Then put it out of reach of danger."

"Where?"

"I am going over to the county town, where there is a bank. Deposit it there, and whenever you want any, go and get it."

"But banks break sometimes," said Ben, in alarm.

"This is an old, established institution. You need not be afraid of it. Even if there is some danger, there is far less than here."

"But I can't see the money—I can't count it," objected Ben.

"You can see the deposit record in a book. Even if that doesn't suit you as well, you can sleep comfortably, knowing that you are not liable to be attacked and murdered by burglars."

The old man vacillated, but finally yielded to the force of the doctor's reasoning. A day or two later he rode over to the neighboring town, and saw his precious gold deposited in the vaults of the bank. He heaved a sigh as it was locked up, but on the whole was tolerably reconciled to the step he had taken.

We are anticipating, however.

When the confusion incident to the arrest was over, Tony came forward.

"Mr. Hayden," he said, "you are so much better that I think you can spare me now."

"But," said the old man, startled at the boy's question, "suppose Rudolph comes back."

"I don't think he can. He will be put in prison."

"I suppose he will. What a bold, bad man."

"Yes, he is a bad man, but I am sorry for him. I don't like to think of one I have been with so long in the walls of a prison. I suppose it can't be helped, though."

"How did you come to be with him?" asked the old man, in a tone of interest.

"I don't know. I have been with him as long as I can remember. You used to know him, didn't you?"

"A little," said the old man, hastily.

"Where was it?"

"In England—long ago."

"In England. Was he born in England?" asked Tony, in surprise.

"Yes."

"And you, too?"

"Yes, I am an Englishman."

"Do you think I am English, too?" asked the boy, eagerly.

"I think so; yes, I think so," answered Ben, cautiously.

"Have you any idea who I am—who were my parents?"

"No, I don't know," said Ben, slowly.

"Can you guess?"

"Don't trouble me now," said Ben, peevishly. "I am not well. My head is confused. Some day I will think it over and tell you what I know."

"But if I am not here?"

"I will write it down and give it to the doctor."

"That will do," said Tony. "I know he will keep it for me, Now, good-by."

"Are you going?"

"Yes, I have my own way to make in the world. I can't live on you any longer."

"To be sure not," said Ben, hastily. "I am too poor to feed two persons, and you have a very large appetite."

"Yes," said Tony, laughing, "I believe I have a healthy appetite. I'm growing, you know."

"It must be that," said old Ben, with the air of one to whom a mystery had just been made clear. "What is your name?"

"Tony," answered our hero, in surprise at the question.

"No. I mean your full name."

"That is more than I know. I have always been called Tony, or Tony the Tramp. Rudolph's last name is Rugg, and he pretends that I am his son. If I were, I should be Tony Rugg."

"You are not his son. He never had any son."

"I am glad to hear that. I shan't have to say now that my father is in jail for robbery. Good-by, Mr. Hayden."

"Good-by," said Ben, following the boy thoughtfully with his eyes till he had disappeared round a turn in the road.

"Well," thought Tony, "I've set up for myself now in earnest. Rudolph can't pursue me, and there is no one else to interfere with me. I must see what fortune waits me in the great world.

With a light heart, and a pocket still lighter, Tony walked on for several miles. Then he stopped at a country grocery store, and bought five cents worth of crackers. These he ate with a good appetite, slaking his thirst at a wayside spring.

He was lying carelessly on the green sward, when a tin peddler's cart drove slowly along the road.

"Hallo, there!" said the peddler.

"Hallo!" said Tony.

"Are you travelin'?"

"Yes."

"Do you want a lift?"

"Yes," said Tony, with alacrity.

"Then get up here. There's room enough for both of us, You can hold the reins when I stop anywhere."

"It's a bargain," said Tony.

"Are you travelin' for pleasure?" asked the peddler, who was gifted with his share of curiosity.

"On business," said Tony.

"What is your business? You're too young for an agent."

"I want to find work," said Tony.

"You're a good, stout youngster. You'd ought to get something to do."

"So I think," said Tony.

"Ever worked any?"

"No."

"Got any folks?"

"If you mean wife and children, I haven't," answered our hero, with a smile.

"Ho, ho!" laughed the peddler. "I guess not. I mean father or mother, uncles or aunts, and such like."

"No, I am alone in the world."

"Sho! you don't say so. Well, that's a pity. Why, I've got forty-'leven cousins and a mother-in-law to boot. I'll sell her cheap."

"Never mind!" said Tony. "I won't deprive you of her."

"I'll tell you what," said the peddler, "I feel interested in you. I'll take you round with me for a day or two, and maybe I can get you a place. What do you say?"

"Yes, and thank you," said Tony.

"Then it's settled. Gee up, Dobbin!"

CHAPTER XIII.

TONY GETS A PLACE.

TOWARD the close of the next day the tin-peddler halted in front of a country tavern, situated in a village of moderate size.

"I'm going to stay here over night," he said.

"Maybe they'll let me sleep in the barn," said Tony.

"In the barn! Why not in the house?"

"I haven't got any money, you know, Mr. Bickford."

"What's the odds? They won't charge anything extra for you to sleep with me."

"You're very kind, Mr. Bickford, but they won't keep me for nothing, and I don't want you to pay for me."

At this moment the landlord came out on the piazza, and asked the hostler:

"Where's Sam?"

"Gone home—says he's sick," answered James.

"Drat that boy! It's my opinion he was born lazy. That's what's the matter with him."

"I guess you're right, Mr. Porter," said James. "The boy don't earn his salt."

"I wouldn't take him back if I had anybody to take his place."

"Do you hear that, Tony?" said the peddler, nudging our hero.

Tony was quick to take the hint.

He walked to the landlord, and said:

"I'll take his place."

"Who are you?" asked the landlord, in surprise. "I never saw you before."

"I have just come," said Tony. "I am looking for a place."

"What can you do?"

"Anything you want me to do."

"Have you any references?"

"I can refer to him," said Tony, pointing to the tin peddler."

"Oh, Mr. Bickford," said the landlord, with a glance of recognition. "Well, that's enough. I'll take you. James, take this boy to the kitchen, and give him some supper. Then tell him what's to be done. What's your name, boy?"

"Tony Rugg."

"Very well, Tony, I'll give you three dollars a week and your board as long as we suit each other."

"I've got into business sooner than I expected," thought Tony."

The hostler set him to work in the barn, and though he was new to the work, he quickly understood what was wanted, and did it.

"You work twice as fast as Sam," said the hostler, approvingly.

"Won't Sam be mad when he finds I have taken his place?" asked Tony.

"Probably he will, but it's his own fault."

"Not if he's sick."

"He's no more sick than I am.   He only wants to get a day or two off.

"Well, I'm glad he left a vacancy for me," said Tony.

"Where did you work last?" asked the hostler.

"Nowhere."

"Never worked?   Then how did you live?"

"I traveled with my guardian."

"Were you rich?" asked James, rather impressed by Tony's answer.

"No; I just went round and lived as I could.   I didn't like it, but I couldn't help it.   I had to go where Rudolph chose to lead me."

"Where is he now?"

"I don't know.   I got tired of being a tramp, and ran away from him.

"You did right," said James, who was a steady man, and looked forward to a snug home of his own ere long.   "All the same, Mr. Porter wouldn't have taken you if he had known you were a tramp."

"I hope you won't tell him, then.   I don't want to be a tramp any longer."

"No; I won't tell him.   I want you to stay here. I'd rather have you than Sam."

"Thank you.   I'll try to suit."

Tony was assigned to a room in the attic.   There were two beds in this chamber, one being occupied by James.   He slept soundly, and was up betimes in the morning.   After breakfast, Mr. Bickford, the tin peddler, made ready to start.

"Good-by, Tony," he said, in a friendly manner. "I'm glad you've got a place."

"I wouldn't have got it if I hadn't you to refer to," said Tony.

"The landlord didn't ask how long I'd known you," said Bickford, smiling. "However, I guess I know enough of you to give you a recommend. Good luck to you."

As the peddler drove away, Tony noticed a big, overgrown boy, who was just entering the hotel yard.

"That's Sam," said the hostler. "He don't know he's lost his place."

CHAPTER XIV.

TONY'S RIVAL.

SAM was about two inches taller than Tony, red haired and freckled, with a big frame, loosely put together. He was a born bully; and many were the tricks he had played on smaller boys in the vil-lage. He liked his place at the hotel because he was no longer obliged to go to school; but he was too lazy to fulfill the duties satisfactorily. His father was a blacksmith, of surly disposition, very much like Sam's, who was generally believed to ill-treat his wife, a meek, uncomplaining woman, who filled the position of a household drudge.

Sam strutted into the yard with the air of a pro-prietor. He took no particular notice of Tony, but accosted James. The latter made a signal to Tony to be silent.

"Well, have you just got along?" asked the hostler.

"Ye-es," drawled Sam.

"What made you go home yesterday afternoon, and not come back?"

"I didn't feel well," said Sam, nonchalantly.

"What was the matter with you?"

"I had a sort of headache."

"Do you think Mr. Porter can afford to pay you

wages and let you go home three times a week in the middle of the afternoon?"

"I couldn't work when I was sick of course," said Sam.

"You're mighty delicate, getting sick two or three times a week."

"Couldn't help it," said Sam, unconcerned.

"I suppose you have come to work this morning?"

"Ye-es, but I can't work very hard—I ain't quite got over my headache."

"Then you'll be glad to hear that you won't have to work at all."

"Ain't there anything to do?" asked Sam, with an air of relief.

"Yes, there's plenty to do, but your services ain't required. You're discharged!"

"What!" exclaimed Sam, his eyes lighting up with anger?

"Mr. Porter's got tired of your delicate health; it interferes too much with business. He's got a tougher boy to take your place."

"Where is he?" demanded Sam, with an ominous frown.

"There," answered the hostler, pointing out our hero, who stood quietly listening to the conversation.

Sam regarded Tony with a contemptuous scowl. So this was the boy who had superseded him. He hated him already for his presumption in venturing to take his place.

"Who are you?" he demanded, roughly.

"Your successor," answered Tony, coolly.

He knew that his answer would make Sam very angry, but he was not afraid of him, and felt under no particular obligations to be polite.

"You won't be my successor long," retorted Sam.

"Why not?"

"What business had you to take my place?"

"The landlord hired me."

"I don't care if he did. He hired me first."

"Then you'd better go to him and complain about it. It's none of my business——"

"It's *my* business," said Sam, with emphasis.

"Just as you like."

"Will you give up the place?"

"No," said Tony. "You must think I'm a fool. What should I give it up for?"

"Because it belongs to me."

"I don't see that; I suppose Mr. Porter has a right to hire anybody he likes."

"He had no right to give you my place."

"That's his business. What shall I do next, James?"

"Go to the barn and shake down some hay for the horses."

"All right."

Sam walked off, deeply incensed, muttering threats of vengeance against Tony.

Three days later a boy entered the stable, and calling for Tony, presented the following missive:

"If you ain't a coward, meet me to-morrow night at seven o'clock, back of the school house, and we'll settle, by fighting, which shall have the place, you or I. If you get whipped, you must clear out, and leave it to me.

"Sam Payson."

Tony showed the note to the hostler.

"Well, Tony, what are you going to do about it?" asked James, curiously.

"I'll be on hand," said Tony, promptly. "He won't find it so easy to whip me as he thinks."

CHAPTER XV.

THE BOYS' DUEL.

SAM PAYSON felt perfectly safe in challenging Tony to single combat. He had measured him with his eye, and seen that he was two inches shorter, and probably twenty pounds lighter. But appearances were deceitful, and he had no idea that Tony had received special training, which he lacked.

This was the way it had happened:

In the course of his extensive wanderings, Tony had attracted the attention of a certain pugilist who was a friend of Rudolph.

"I'll tell you what, Rudolph," said the pugilist, "you can make something of that boy."

"How?" asked the tramp.

"I'll teach him to box, and you can get an engagement for him in a circus."

"Do it if you like," said the tramp. "It won't do him any harm."

"So Tony received a gratuitous course of lessons in boxing, which were at last interrupted by a little difficulty between his teacher and the officers of the law, resulting in the temporary confinement of the former. The lessons were never resumed, but they had gone so far that Tony was quite a skillful boxer for a boy.

He, too, had measured Sam, and felt quite sure of being able to conquer him, and that with ease. He did not, however, mention the grounds of his confidence to James, when the latter expressed some apprehension that he would find Sam too much for him.

"Don't be alarmed, James," said Tony, quietly. "I'm enough for him."

"He's bigger than you," said James.

"I know that, but he's clumsy."

"He's slow, but he's pretty strong."

"So am I."

"You've got pluck, and you deserve to beat, Tony," said his friend.

"I mean to," answered Tony. "Come along and see that it's all fair."

"I will if I can get away. Will you give up your place if you are licked?"

"Yes," replied Tony, "I'll give up my place and leave the village."

"I don't believe Mr. Porter will take Sam back."

"I see you are expecting I will be whipped," said Tony, laughing; "but you're mistaken. Sam isn't able to do it."

James feared that Tony overestimated his prowess, but earnestly hoped that the boy, in whom he already felt a strong interest, would achieve the victory.

Meanwhile, Sam had made known the duel which was about to take place. He confidently anticipated victory, and wanted the village boys to be witnesses of the manner in which he was going to polish off that interloper.

"I'll learn him to cut me out of my place," he said, boastfully; "I'll learn him to mind his own business."

"Will you get your place again if you lick him?" asked one of his companions.

"Of course I will."

"Suppose he won't give it up?"

"Then I'll lick him every day till he's glad to clear out. All you boys know I don't stand no nonsense."

The result of Sam's boastful talk was that about a hundred boys collected about the school house to witness the boys' duel.

Many of them who had suffered from Sam's bullying disposition would have been glad to see him worsted, but none anticipated it.

Nothing was known of Tony except that he was considerably smaller and lighter, and probably weaker. It was generally thought that he would not be able to hold out long, and that Sam would achieve an easy victory.

Tony tried to be on hand at the time appointed, but he had more than usual to do, and it was five minutes past seven when he entered the field, accompanied by James.

There had been various speculations as to the cause of his delay.

"He won't come," said Sam, with a sneer; he's afraid."

"What'll you do if he don't come?" asked John Nolan.

"What will I do? I'll pitch into him wherever I see him."

"Didn't he accept your challenge?"

"Yes, he accepted, but he's thought better of it, likely."

"There he comes!" shouted a small boy.

All eyes were turned upon Tony, as he entered the field, with James at his side.

"I'm sorry to have kept you waiting, boys," said our hero, politely.

"We concluded you'd backed out," said Sam, with a sneer.

"That isn't my style," returned Tony, with a quiet smile. "I had more to do than usual to-night."

"You've still more to do," said Sam, jeeringly. "I pity you."

"Do you? You're very kind," said Tony, unmoved.

"Oh, don't thank me too soon?"

"Then I won't. When are the exercises to commence?"

"He takes it cool," said Nolan.

"Oh, it's only show off," said Sam. "You'll see how he'll wilt down when I get hold of him."

The two boys stripped off coat and vest, and faced each other. Tony was wary and watchful, and quietly looked into the eyes of his adversary, showing no disposition to begin.

Sam began business by thrusting his right fist violently in his face, or rather trying to do so. With scarcely an effort Tony parried the blow, and returned it quick as lightning, striking Sam full in the nose.

Sam was not only maddened, but disagreeably surprised, especially when he discovered that blood was trickling from the injured organ. He was still more incensed by the murmur of applause which followed from the crowd of boys. Had the applause been elicited by his success, he would have enjoyed it, but now it was quite a different matter.

He breathed an audible curse, and, losing all prudence, began to let drive at Tony with each fist in rapid succession, with the intention of overpowering him. But, unfortunately for him, this exposed him to attack, and a couple of forcible blows in his face warned him that this was too dangerous.

Tony stood upright, as cool and collected as at first. He had warded off every blow of his adversary, and thus far was untouched.

There was a murmur of surprise among the boys. They had come to see Tony used up, and all the using up had proved to be from the other side. James was as much delighted as surprised. He could not repress clapping his hands, a movement which was quickly imitated by the boys.

"Tony knows how to take care of himself," he thought. "That's why he took matters so coolly. I didn't half believe him when he told me there was no danger."

Sam felt humiliated and maddened. He regretted now that he had undertaken a task which seemed every moment more formidable. What! was it possible that he, Sam Payson, the crack fighter of the village, was being ignominiously whipped, and that by a smaller boy. He felt that if he permitted this his prestige would be forever gone, and with it the influence which he so much prized. He must make one desperate effort.

"If I can only get hold of him," he thought, 'I, can shake the life out of him."

He tried to grasp Tony round the body, intending to throw him violently down upon the ground; but our hero was too quick for him, and showered the blows upon him with such rapidity that, blinded and overwhelmed, Sam himself fell on his back.

Instead of following up the victory, Tony drew off and let his adversary rise. Sam renewed the attack so wildly that in two minutes he was again lying flat.

"'That's enough, Sam! You're whipped," shouted the boys.

But Sam was not convinced. He renewed the attacked once more, but there was no hope for him now.

He got up sullenly, and, in a voice nearly choked with rage, said:

"I'll be even with you yet, see if I don't."

"Hurrah for the stranger!" shouted the boys enthusiastically, as they crowded around our hero.

"Boys," said Tony, modestly, "I'm much obliged

to you for your congratulations.   Was it a fair
fight?"

"Yes, yes."

"Then's it all right.   Don't say anything to him
about it.   He feels bad, as I should do in his place.
I haven't any ill will toward him, and I hope he
hasn't toward me."

This speech made Tony a still greater favorite
and the boys, making a rush, took him on their
shoulders, and bore him in triumph to the inn. Poor
Sam slunk home, suffering keener mortification
than he had ever before experienced in his life.

CHAPTER XVI.

RUDOLPH ESCAPES AND SEES AN ADVERTISEMENT.

LEAVING Tony for a short time, we must return to Rudolph, whom we left in charge of a self-constituted body of police on his way to the station-house.

Of course there was no regular prison in the village. There was not properly even a station-house. But under the engine house was a basement room, which was used as a lock-up. It was not often used, for few rogues of a serious character disturbed the tranquility of the village. Occasionally a man was put in who had disturbed the peace while under the influence of liquor, but even such cases were rare.

When first arrested Rudolph was disposed to be violent and abusive. His disappointment was keen, for he was just congratulating himself on the possession of the miser's gold. Five minutes later, and he would probably have been able to make good his escape. Mingled with his disappointment was a feeling of intense hostility against Tony for his part in defeating his plans.

"I'll be revenged upon him yet," he muttered between his teeth.

"What did you say?" asked one of his captors.

"Nothing," answered Rudolph.

"I thought I heard you say something."

"I said I was tired."

"Then you will have a chance to rest in the lock-up."

Rudolph frowned, but said nothing.

They reached the lockup. The door was opened, and he was led in. A small oil lamp was lighted, and set on the floor.

"Where are the handcuffs?" asked one of the captors.

"I don't know. They haven't been needed for so long that they have been mislaid."

"They won't be needed now. The man can't get out."

Rudolph's face betrayed satisfaction, but he thought it prudent to say nothing.

"There's your bed," says Moses Hunt, who had Rudolph by the arm, pointing to a rude cot in the corner.

Rudolph threw himself upon it.

"I'm dead tired," he said, and closed his eyes.

"He'll be quiet enough. We can leave him alone," said Hunt.

"All right."

The door was locked, and Rudolph was left alone.

When five minutes had elapsed—time enough for his captors to get away—he rose in bed, and looked about him.

Beside the bed in which he was lying there was no other furniture in the room than a wooden chair.

He got up and walked about.

"I must get away from this if I can," thought the tramp, "and before morning. I am glad they didn't put on handcuffs. Let me see, how shall I manage it."

He looked about him thoughtfully.

It was a basement room, lighted only by windows three feet wide and a foot high in the upper part of the room.

"I should like to set fire to the building, and burn it up," thought the tramp. "That would cost them something. But it wouldn't be safe. Like as not I would be burnt up myself, or, at any rate, be taken again in getting away. No, no; that won't do."

"I wonder if I can get through one of those windows?" was the next thought that came into his mind.

He stood on the chair, and as the room was low-slatted he found he could easily reach the windows in question.

He shook them, and found to his joy that it would be a comparatively easy thing to remove one of them.

"What fools they are," he muttered contemptuously. "Did they really expect to keep me here. They must think I am a green hand."

He removed the window, and by great effort succeeded in raising himself so that he might have a chance of drawing himself through the aperture. It did not prove so easy as he expected. He did, however, succeed at length, and drew a long breath of satisfaction as he found himself once more in the possession of his liberty.

"I'm a free man once more," he said. "What next?"

He would have been glad to return to the miser's house, and possessed himself of some of his gold, but the faint gray of dawn was already perceptible, and there was too much risk attending it. He felt that this must be deferred to a more fitting occasion.

A few days later the tramp found himself in the streets of New York.

For the time he had given up the pursuit of Tony. Indeed, he had wholly lost the clew. Moreover, prudence dictated his putting as great a distance as possible between himself and the village where he had been arrested.

The hundred miles intervening between New York and that place he had got over in his usual way, begging a meal at one house, and a night's lodging at another. He was never at a loss for a plausible story. At one place where he was evidently looked upon with suspicion, he said:

"I aint used to beggin'. I'm a poor, hard-workin' man, but I've heard that my poor daughter is sick in New York, and she's in the hospital. Poor girl! I'm afraid she'll suffer."

" What took her to New York?" asked the farmer whom he addressed.

"She went to take a place in a store," said Rudolph readily, "but she's been taken sick, and she's in the hospital. Poor girl! I'm afraid she'll suffer."

"I'm sorry for you," said the farmer's wife, sympathizingly. "Ephraim, can't we help along this poor man?"

"If we can believe him. There's many impostors about."

"I hope you don't take me for one," said Rudolph, meekly. "Poor Jane; what would she think if she knew how poor father was so misunderstood."

"Poor man! I believe you," said the farmer's wife. "You shall sleep in Jonathan's bed. He's away now."

So Rudolph was provided with two abundant meals and a comfortable bed. The farmer's wife never doubted his story, though she could not help feeling that his looks were not prepossessing. But, was her charitable thought, the poor man can't help his looks.

Of course Rudolph had been in New York often, and his familiar haunts. As a general thing, however, he shunned the city, for he was already known to the police, and he felt that watchful eyes would be upon him as soon as it was known that he was back again.

On the second day he strolled into a low drinking place in the lower part of the city.

A man in shirt sleeves, and with unhealthy complexion, was mixing drinks behind the bar.

"Hallo, Rudolph! Back again?" was his salutation.

"Yes," said the tramp, throwing himself down in a seat.

"What's the news with you? Been prospering?"

"No."

"Where have you been?"

"Tramping round the country."

"Where's the boy you used to have with you?"

"Run away; curse him!" returned the tramp with a fierce scowl."

"Got tired of your company, eh?"

"He wants to be honest and respectable," answered Rudolph, with a sneer.

"And he thought he could learn better under another teacher, did he?" said the bartender, with a laugh.

"Yes, I suppose so. I'd like to wring his neck," muttered the tramp.

"You're no friend to the honest and respectable, then?"

"No, I'm not."

"Then, there's no love lost, for they don't seem to fancy you. What'll you have to drink?"

"I've got no money."

"I'll trust. You'll have some some time?"

"Give me some whisky, then," said the tramp.

The whisky was placed in his hands. He gulped it down, and breathed a sigh of satisfaction.

Then resuming his seat, he took up a morning paper. At first he read it listlessly, but soon his face assumed a look of eager interest.

This was the paragraph that arrested his attention:

"Should this meet the eye of Rudolph Rugg, who

left England in the fall of 1857, he is requested to communicate with Jacob Morris, attorney-at-law, Room 11, No. —, Nassau street."

Rudolph rose hurriedly.

" Going?" asked the bartender.

" Yes; I'll be back again soon."

CHAPTER XVII.

THE LADY AT THE ST. NICHOLAS.

WHEN Rudolph reached the sidewalk he stopped a moment to reflect on the probable meaning of the advertisement.

"Perhaps it is a trap," he thought. "Perhaps, after so many years, they want to punish me. Shall I go?"

His hesitation was only temporary.

"There's nothing to be afraid of," he concluded. "Very likely I shall hear something to my advantage. I will go."

Ten minutes' walk brought him to Nassau street. He ascended two flights of stairs, opened the door of No. —, and found himself in a lawyer's office. A tall man of forty was seated at a desk, with some papers and books lying before him.

"Well," he said inquiringly, "what can I do for you, sir?"

The address was not very cordial, for Rudolph did not have the look of one likely to be a profitable client.

"Are you Mr. Jacob Morris, attorney-at-law?" asked the tramp.

"That is my name."

"I am Rudolph Rugg."

"Rudolph Rugg!" exclaimed the lawyer, briskly, jumping from his chair, "you don't say so. I am very glad to see you. Take a chair, please."

Reassured by this reception, Rudolph took the seat indicated.

"So you saw my advertisement?" said the lawyer, brushing away the papers with which he had been occupied.

"Yes, sir. I only saw it this morning."

"It has been inserted for the last two weeks, daily. How happens it that you did not see it sooner?"

"I have been away from the city. I have been traveling. It was only an accident that I happened to see it to-day."

"A lucky accident, Mr. Rugg."

"I hope it is, sir, for I have been out of luck myself, and I've been hoping something would turn up for me. What is the business, sir?"

"My business has been to find you. I can't say anything more."

"To find me?"

"Yes."

"What for?"

"For a client of mine—an English lady."

"A lady?" ejaculated the tramp, with unconcealed surprise.

"Yes."

"Who is it?"

"I suppose I am at liberty to tell. The lady is Mrs. Harvey Middleton, of Middleton Hall, England."

A peculiar expression swept over Rudolph's face, but he only said:

"I have heard the name of Harvey Middleton. Is—is the lady in New York?"

"Yes; she is staying at the St. Nicholas Hotel."

"And she wants to find me?"

"Yes, she authorized me to seek you out."

"Well," said Rudolph, after a brief pause, "I'm found. "What next?"

"I shall at once send a messenger to Mrs. Middleton, and await her orders. You will stay here."

He went to the door and called "John," in a loud voice.

"Look here," said Rudolph, suspiciously, "just tell me one thing. There ain't any trap is there?"

"Trap, my good friend? What can you possibly mean?"

"You ain't sending for the police?"

"To be sure not. Besides, why should a gentleman like you fear the police?"

"Oh, that's all gammon. I do fear the police uncommon. But if you tell me it's all on the square, I'll believe you."

"On my honor, then, it's all on the square, as you call it. No harm whatever is designed you. Indeed, I have reason to think that you will make considerable money out of it. Now, hark ye, my friend, a word in confidence. We can do each other good."

"Can we?" asked the tramp, surveying the lawyer, in surprise.

"Yes, and I'll tell you how. This lady, Mrs. Middleton, appears to be rich."

"She is rich."

"So much the better for us. I mean to give her the idea that I have been at great trouble and expense in finding you."

"I see," said Rudolph, smiling. "You mean to charge it in the bill."

"Of course, I shall represent that I sent out messengers in search of you, and you were found by one of them."

"Very good."

"So you need not say anything about the advertisement."

"All right, sir."

"Grant me a moment while I pencil a note to the lady."

    *   *   *   *   *   *   *

In a private parlor at the St. Nicholas sat a lady of middle age. She had a haughty face, and stern, compressed lips. She was one to repel rather than to attract. She had a note before her, which she threw down with an exclamation of impatience.

"So he has heard nothing yet. For three weeks I have been wasting my time at this hotel, depending on this lawyer, and he has done absolutely nothing. And the issue is so important. I may have to employ another person, and that will be a fresh bill of expense."

At this moment a light knock was heard at the door.

"Enter," said the lady.

"A note for Mrs. Middleton," announced a servant.

She took the missive and hastily opened it. It read thus:

"MY DEAR MADAM—At last, after unwearied exertions, I have succeeded. The man, Rudolph Rugg, has been found by one of my messengers, and is at this moment in my office, ready to obey your summons. Shall I send him to you?

> "Yours, respectfully,
> > "JACOB MORRIS."

"P. S.—I assured you at the outset that if he were living I would find him. I am sure you will appreciate my exertions in your behalf."

"That means a larger bill," thought the lady. "However, I am willing to pay handsomely. The man is found, and he can, doubtless, produce the boy."

"Wait!" she said, in an imperious tone, to the servant, who was about to withdraw. "There is an answer."

She hastily penciled the following note:

"I am very glad you have found Rudolph Rugg. I wish to speak to him at once. Send him here directly."

"Short and not sweet!" commented the lawyer, when it was placed in his hands. "She says nothing about the compensation."

"Is it about me?" asked the tramp, watching the lawyer's face eagerly.

"Yes; it is from Mrs. Middleton. She wants you to come to the hotel at once. But, my friend, if you will excuse the suggestion, I would advise you, since you are about to call upon a lady, to put on a better suit of clothes."

The tramp scowled at the hint.

"How am I to do it," he demanded roughly, "when these are all the clothes I have?"

The lawyer whistled.

"A pretty looking figure to call upon a lady at a fashionable hotel!" he thought.

"You must go as you are," he said. "Wait a minute."

He took a blank card and wrote upon it the name:

RUDOLPH RUGG.

"When you reach the hotel," he said, "inquire for Mrs. Middleton, and send that card up to her."

"Very well, sir."

The tramp started for the hotel, his mind busily occupied.

"What does she want with me? She wasn't Mrs. Middleton when I knew her; she was Miss Vincent, the governess. I suppose she's a great lady now. So she got Mr. Harvey to marry her. That ain't surprisin'. She looked like a schemer even then, and I was a fool not to see what she was at. Likely she was up to the other thing. Well, I shall soon know."

CHAPTER XVIII.

TWO CONSPIRATORS.

"You want to see Mrs. Middleton?" demanded the hotel clerk, surveying Mr. Rugg's exterior with a glance which betokened suspicion.

"Yes," said the tramp.

"I don't think she'll see one of your sort."

"That's where you're mistaken, young feller,' said Rudolph, loftily. "She wants to see me uncommon."

"You're a strange visitor for a lady."

"What if I am? There's my card. Just you send it up, and see if she won't see me."

The clerk took the card, and looked at it doubtfully. Then summoning an attendant, he said:

"Take this up to 57."

Presently the servant returned.

"The gentleman is to go up," he said.

Rudolph looked at the clerk triumphantly.

"What did I tell you?" he said.

"Show the *gentleman* up," said the clerk, purposely emphasizing the word.

As Rudolph entered the handsome parlor occupied by Mrs. Middleton, she said:

"Take a seat, sir." Then to the attendant: "You may go. You are Rudolph Rugg?" she commenced when they were alone.

"Yes, ma'am," he answered; "and you are Miss Vincent, the governess. I haven't forgotten you."

"I am Mrs Harvey Middleton," she said haughtily.

"Excuse me, ma'am. I hadn't heard as you had changed your condition. You was the governess when I knowed you."

"You never knew me," she said, in the same haughty tone.

"Well, I knowed Mr. Harvey, at any rate."

"That is not to the purpose. Do you know why I have sought you out?"

"I couldn't guess, ma'am," said Rudolph, cunningly.

He could guess, but he wanted to force her to speak out.

"Where is the boy? Is he living?" she demanded, eagerly.

"What boy?" asked Rudolph, vacantly.

"You know very well. Robert Middleton, my husband's cousin, whom you stole away when he was scarcely more than an infant."

"Can you prove what you say, Miss Vincent—I mean Mrs. Middleton?"

"Yes. It is idle to beat about the bush. My husband has told me all."

"Then he has told you that he hired me to carry the boy off, in order that he might inherit the estate?"

The tramp looked searchingly in the lady's face as he said this.

"Yes, he told me that," she answered, composedly.

"Well, I didn't think he'd own up to that," said the tramp, in surprise.

"My husband and I had no secrets," said the lady, coldly.

"What does he want of the boy now?" asked Rudolph.

"It is I that want to find the boy."

"Without his knowledge?"

"If you refer to my husband, he is dead."

"Dead! You don't say so?"

"He died six months ago."

"Well, I didn't expect that. Who has got the estate?"

"I have."

The tramp whistled, and surveyed the lady with genuine admiration. Here was a poor governess, who had succeeded in life with a vengeance. When he knew her she was not worth fifty pounds in the world. Now she was a mistress of a fine English estate, with a rental of two thousand pounds.

"Wasn't there no heirs?" he asked.

"Only this boy."

"And if this boy was alive would the estate be his?"

The lady paused, meanwhile fixing her eyes steadily upon the man before her. Then, as if rapidly making up her mind, she approached him, and placed her jeweled hand on his arm.

"Rudolph Rugg," she said, "do you want to be comfortable for life?"

"Yes, ma'am, that's exactly what I do want. I've been wanting it ever since I was old enough to know the power of money, but it has never come to me."

"It will come to you now if you say the word," she said.

"I'll say it quick enough. Tell me what you want."

"You talk like a sensible man. But first tell me, is the boy living?"

"He is alive and well."

She frowned slightly, as if the intelligence didn't please her.

"Do you know where he is?"

"Yes," answered Rudolph.

It was false, of course, but he thought it was for his interest to answer in the affirmative.

"When did you see him last?"

"Last week."

"Very well, you know where he is. That is important. Now, in order that you may understand what service I want of you, I must tell you a little of my circumstances. I told you that my husband left me the estate."

"Yes, ma'am."

"But only in trust."

"For the boy?" asked the tramp, in excitement.

"Precisely."

"Well, I'll be blowed."

"What excites you, Mr. Rugg?"

"To think that Tony, the tramp, should be the

owner of a splendid estate in old Hingland, and not know anything about it."

"I am the owner," said the lady, frowning.

"But you're only takin' care of it for him."

"I don't mean that he shall ever know it."

Rudolph whistled.

"I wish you would forbear whistling in the presence of a lady. It is unmannerly," said Mrs. Middleton, annoyed.

"I ain't much used to associating with ladies," said the tramp.

"Bear it it in mind, then." she said, sharply. "Now to business."

"Yes, ma'am, to business."

"My husband secured the inheritance, as you are aware, through the disappearance of his young cousin. And mighty well he managed it."

"But after he fell into ill health, and was given over by the doctors, he became a prey to superstitious fears, the result of his weakness, and at times experienced great regret for the hand he had in the abduction of the boy."

"You surprise me, ma'am. He wasn't that sort when I knew him."

"No; he was then in perfect health, and was bold and resolute. Ill health and the approach of death made him superstitious."

"You ain't that way, ma'am, I take it," said Rudolph, with a leer.

"No; I have a stronger will and greater resolution, I hope."

Her face did not belie her words. There was a cold look in her light-gray eyes, and a firmness in her closely-pressed lips, which made it clear that she was not likely to be affected by ordinary weakness. She was intensely selfish, and thoroughly unscrupulous as to the means which she employed to carry out her selfish ends.

"So you're afraid the boy'll turn up, ma'am?" asked Rudolph.

"Precisely."

"Then why do you look for him?"

"I want to guard against his ever turning up. I hoped you would be able to tell me he was dead."

"He don't know about the property."

"But he might have learned, or you might. My husband, with the idea of reparation, left the property to me, in trust, but if it should ever be fully ascertained that the boy had died, then it was to be mine absolutely. There must be clear proof."

"I begin to see what you're driving at, ma'am."

"You say the boy is alive?"

"Yes, ma'am."

"And well?"

"Stout and hearty, ma'am. He's been under my care ever since he was a young 'un, ma'am, and I've treated him like he was my own."

"Indeed!"

"Yes, ma'am. I'm poor, but I've always shared my crust with him, givin' him the biggest half."

"Very kind, I'm sure," said the lady, sarcastically. "I suppose you're very fond of him."

" Of course I am," said Rudolph, "but," he added, after a slight pause, " there's one thing I like better."

" What is that? "

"Money."

" Good!" said the lady, her face lighting up with satisfaction. "I see we understand one another."

"That's so, ma'am. You needn't be afraid to say anything to me. Business is business."

" Draw your chair near mine, Mr. Rugg," said Mrs. Middleton, affably.

The tramp did so. He foresaw what was coming, but did not flinch.

CHAPTER XIX.

THE WICKED COMPACT.

"It appears to me, Mr. Rugg, that you have prospered," said the lady.

"That's where you're right, ma'am, and you couldn't be righter."

"I'm as poor as I can be."

"So am I," said the tramp, adding, with a cunning look, "but times will be better now."

"Why will they be better?" asked Mrs. Middleton, suspiciously.

"Tony won't see me want when he comes into ten thousand a year."

"Who said he was coming into it?" demanded the lady, coldly.

"You said he was the heir."

"He hasn't got the estate, and I don't mean he shall have it."

"How will you prevent that ma'am?"

Mrs. Middleton again put her hand on the man's tattered coat sleeve, and in a voice scarcely above a whisper, said:

"Mr. Rugg, you must prevent it."

"How can I prevent it?" asked the tramp, with an assumption of innocence.

"I take it, you are not a religious man?"

"Not much," answered the tramp, with a short laugh.

"You are not afraid—to do wrong?"

"Yes, I am, ma'am; but if I was paid for it I might not mind."

"You shall be paid, and paid well."

"What do you want me to do?"

Mrs. Middleton said, with slow significance:

"This boy is in my way. Don't you think he might manage to get sick and die?"

"Perhaps he might," said Rudolph, who did not appear to be shocked at the suggestion.

"Couldn't you manage it?" she asked, her eyes fixed upon the tramp.

"I might," he answered, shrewdly, "if it was going to do me any good."

"Then the only question is as to pay," she continued.

"That's about it ma'am. It's a big risk, you know. I might get caught, and then money wouldn't do me much good."

"Nothing venture, nothing have. You don't want to be a pauper all your life?"

"No, I don't, answered the tramp with energy. "I'm tired of tramping round the country, sleeping in barns and under hay-stacks, and picking up meals where I can. I've had enough of it."

"Do as I wish, and you need never suffer such privations again," said the tempter.

"How much will you give me?" asked Rudolph, in a business-like manner.

"Five hundred dollars down and five hundred dollars income as long as you live."

This was good fortune of which Rudolph had never dreamed, but he understood how to make the best of the situation.

"It is not enough," he said, shaking his head.

"Not enough!" exclaimed Mrs. Middleton, with a look of displeasure. "Why, it seems to me very liberal. You can live comfortably all your life just for doing one thing."

"A thing which may bring me to the gallows. It's all very well to talk, but I can't risk my neck for that."

The lady was not surprised. She had expected that she would be compelled to drive a bargain, and and she had named a sum less than she was willing to pay.

"You see," continued Rudolph, "it's going to be a great thing for you. You'll be sure of a big estate and an income of two thousand pounds—that's ten thousand dollars—a year, and it'll be me that gives it to you."

"You overestimate your services, Mr. Rugg," she said, coldly. "If I decline to proceed further the estate will be mine."

"Not if I bring on the boy, and say he's the real heir."

"I shall deny it," said the lady, composedly, "and challenge you to the proof."

"You will?" queried the tramp, disconcerted.

"Of course I shall."

"Then I'll prove it," he continued, in tone of triumph.

"Who will believe you?" asked Mrs. Middleton, quietly.

"Why shouldn't they?"

"You are a tramp, and a discreditable person. Your appearance would be against you. I suspect the boy is one of the same sort."

"No, he isn't. I don't like him overmuch, but he's a handsome chap, looks the gentleman every inch, even if he is dressed a little shabby."

"I should charge you with conspiracy, Mr. Rugg. You'd find it uphill work fighting me without influence and without money. To begin with, how would you get over to England?"

As presented by Mrs. Middleton, certainly the chances did not look flattering.

But an idea occurred to Rudolph, and he instantly expressed it:

"Then, if there ain't no danger from me or the boy, why do you offer me anything to put him out of the way?"

Mrs. Middleton hesitated.

"I may as well tell you," she said, after a moment's pause. "I take it for granted you will keep the matter secret."

"Of course I will."

"Then it is this: I married Mr. Harvey Middleton to secure a home and a position. I didn't love him."

"Quite right, ma'am."

"I was a poor governess. It was a great thing for me to marry Mr. Middleton."

"I should think so."

"I made him a good wife. He had no reason to complain of me, and when he died he left me in charge of the estate."

"For the boy?"

"Yes, for the boy, and this has given me trouble."

"He hasn't never troubled you."

"Not yet, and but for one thing I would not have come to America in search of him."

"What is that?"

"That is the secret I am going to tell you. I want to marry again."

The tramp whistled.

Mrs. Middleton frowned, but went on:

"This time I love the man I want to marry. He is from an excellent family, but he is a younger son, and has little or nothing himself. If the estate were mine absolutely, there would be no opposition on the part of his family to his marrying me to-morrow, but with the knowledge that the boy may turn up at any time, nothing will be done."

"I see," said the tramp, nodding.

"But for this, I never would have stirred in the matter at all. I did not think it probable that the boy would ever hear of his inheritance."

"He don't even know who he is," said Rudolph.

"You never told him, then?" said the lady in a tone of satisfaction.

"No.   What was the good?"

"There was no good, and you did wisely.   Now I have told you how matters stand, and I renew the offer which I made you a few minutes since."

"It is too little," said the tramp, shaking his head."

"Tell me what you expect.   Mind, I don't say that I will meet your views if they are extravagant. Still I might agree to pay you a little more."

"I want just double what you offered me, ma'am."

"Why, that's extortion."

"That's as you choose to consider it, ma'am. It'll leave you money enough.   It's one-tenth.

"Suppose I refuse."

"Then I'll go and see a lawyer, and he'll tell me what I had better do."

"Even if you succeeded, and got the boy in possession, do you think he would give you any more than I offered?"

This was a consideration which had not occurred to the tramp.   He had only thought of punishing the lady for not acceding to his terms.   He asked himself, moreover, did he really wish Tony to come into such a piece of good fortune, and that after the boy had been instrumental in having him arrested. No, anything but that!   He decided to work for Mrs. Middleton, and make the best terms he could."

"I'll tell you what I'll do ma'am," he said.   "I'll say eight hundred dollars down, and the same every year."

To this sum Mrs. Middleton finally agreed.

"You say you know where the boy is?" she asked.

"Yes, ma'am."

"Then there need be no delay."

"Only a little. But I shall want some money. I haven't a penny."

Mrs. Middleton took out her purse.

"Here are a hundred dollars," she said. "The rest shall be paid you when you have earned it."

Rudolph rose to go, and as he went down stairs thoughtfully, he said to himself:

"That woman's a case if ever there was one. How coolly she hires me to kill the boy. I don't half like the job. It's too risky. But there's money in it, and I can't refuse. The first thing is to find him!"

CHAPTER XX.

THE FIGHTING QUAKER.

THE tramp decided that the best way to find Tony would be to return to that part of the country where he had lost him, and make inquiries for a boy of his description.   He could do it more comfortably now, being provided with funds, thanks to Mrs. Middleton.   He was now able to command fair accommodations, and this was satisfactory.

But there was another difficulty which, at times, gave him uneasiness.   He had escaped from the custody of the law, and was liable to be arrested. This would have disconcerted him, and interfered seriously with the purpose he had in view.

"I must disguise myself," thought Rudolph.   "It won't do to run any risk.   When I was a tramp I didn't care, but now I've got something to live for."

It was not the first time in his varied experience that he had felt the need of a disguise, and he knew just where to go to find one.   In the lower part of the city there was a shop well provided with such articles as he required.   He lost no time in seeking it out.

"What can I do for you, Mr. Rugg?" asked the old man who kept the establishment.

"I want a disguise."

"Then you've come to the right shop.   What will you be—a sailor, a Quaker, a—"

" Hold, there," said Rudolph. " You've named the very thing."

" What?"

" A Quaker. Can you make me a good broad-brim?" .

" Yea, verily," answered the old man, laughing, " I can suit thee to a T."

" Do so, then."

From out a pile of costmes of various styles and fashions the old man drew a suit of drab and a broad-brimmed hat.

" How will that do?" he asked.

'·Capital!" answered Rudolph, with satisfaction, "that is, if it will fit."

" I'll answer for that. It's made for a man of your size. Will you try it on?"

" First tell me the price."

" Thirty dollars."

" Thirty dollars!" exclaimed the tramp, aghast. " Do you think I am made of money?"

" Look at the quality, my good friend. Look at the cloth."

" Why, I may not want the things for more than a week."

" Then, I'll tell you what I'll do. If you only use them a week, you shall bring them back, and I will pay you back twenty-five dollars; that is," added the old man cautiously, "if you don't hurt 'em too much."

" That's better," said Rudolph. " I'll try them on."

He went into an inner room, provided for the purpose, and soon came out entirely transformed. In addition to the drab suit, a gray wig had been supplied, which gave him the appearance of a highly respectable old Quaker.

The old man laughed heartily, for he had a merry vein.

"How dost thee like it?" he asked.

"Capital," said Rudolph; "would you know me?"

"I wouldn't dream it was you. But, Mr. Rugg, there's one thing you mustn't forget."

"What's that?"

"To use the Quaker lingo. Just now you said, 'Would you know me?' That isn't right."

"What should I say?"

"Would thee know me?"

"All right. I'll get it after a while. There's your money."

"There you are again. You must say thy money."

"I see you know all about it. You've been a Quaker yourself, haven't you?"

"Not I; but I was brought up in Philadelphia, and I have seen plenty of the old fellows. That's right. Now, don't forget how to talk. Where are you going?"

"Into the country on a little expedition," said Rudolph.

"When will you be back?"

"In a week, if all goes well."

" Well, good luck to you."

" I wish thee good luck, too," said the tramp.

" Ha, ha! You've got it; you'll do."

The tramp emerged into the street, a very fair representative of a sedate Quaker. At first he forgot his gray hair, and walked with a briskness that was hardly in character with his years. He soon attracted the attention of some street boys, who, not suspecting his genuineness, thought him fair game.

"How are you, old Broadbrim?" said one.

Rudolph didn't resent this. He felt rather pleased at this compliment to his get up.

"You'd make a good scarecrow, old buffer," said another.

Still the tramp kept his temper.

A third boy picked up a half-eaten apple and fired it at him.

This was too much for the newly-converted disciple of William Penn.

"Just let me catch you, you little rascal," he exclaimed, "and I'll give you the worst licking you ever had.

The boys stared open mouthed at such language from the sedate old gentlemen.

"He's a fighting Quaker," said the first one, "keep out of his way."

"If thee don't, thee'll catch it," said Rudolph, fortunately remembering how he must talk.

He had thought of pursuing the disturbers of his peace, but motives of prudence prevented him.

CHAPTER XXI.

RUDOLPH HEARS OF TONY.

FOUR days afterward Rudolph arrived in the town where Tony was employed. He had not been drawn thither by any clew, but by pure accident.

He put up for the night at the hotel where our hero had found work. He enrolled himself on the register as "Obadiah Latham, Philadelphia."

This, he thought, would answer very well for a Quaker name, much better, certainly, than Rudolph Rugg, which on other accounts also was objectionable.

"Can thee give me a room, friend?" he inquired at the desk.

"Certainly, sir," was the polite reply. "Here, Henry, show this old gentleman up to No. 6. No. 6 is one of our best rooms, Mr. Latham."

"I thank thee," said the tramp, who, by this time, was quite accustomed to the peculiar phraseology of the Friends.

"The Quakers are always polite," said the book-keeper. They are good pay, too, and never give any trouble. I wish we had more of them stop here."

"If all your customers were of that description, your bar wouldn't pay very well."

"That is true."

"But later in the evening the speaker was obliged to change his opinion.

The Quaker came up to the bar, and asked:

"Will thee give me a glass of brandy?"

"Sir?" said the barkeeper, astounded, and hardly believing his ears.

"A glass of brandy!" repeated Rudolph, irritably. "Where is thy ears?"

"I beg pardon, sir, but I was surprised. I did not know that gentlemen of your faith ever drank liquor."

"Thee is right," said the tramp, recollecting himself. "It is only for my health. Thee may make it strong, so that I may feel better soon."

Rudolph drained the glass, and then after a little hesitation, he said:

"I feel better. Will thee mix me another glass, and a little stronger?"

A stronger glass was given him, and he poured it down rapidly.

The barkeeper looked at him shrewdly.

"Quaker as he is, he is evidently used to brandy," he said to himself. "If he wasn't those two glasses would have upset him."

But Rudolph did not appear to be upset, or, indeed, to be in the least affected.

He put his broad-brimmed hat more firmly on his head, and went outside. He determined to take a walk about the village. This was his usual custom on arriving in a new place. On such occasions he kept his eyes open, and looked about, in the hope that he might somewhere see the object of his search. He little suspected that Tony was at that very moment in the stable-yard in the rear of the hotel.

He walked on for perhaps a quarter of a mile, and then leaned against a fence to rest. As he stood here, two boys passed him slowly, conversing as they walked.

"I was surprised, Sam, at Tony Rugg's whipping you," said the first.

"He couldn't do it again," said Sam, sullenly.

Rudolph's attention was at once drawn.

Tony Rugg! Why, there could be but one Tony Rugg.

He advanced toward the boys.

"Boys," he asked, "did thee mention the name of Tony Rugg?"

"Yes, sir."

"Does thee know such a boy?"

"Yes, sir. He is working at the hotel. He got my place away from me," said Sam. "Do you know him?"

"I once knew such a boy. But no! his name was Charles."

"Perhaps he's a relation."

"Perhaps thee are right."

This the tramp said cunningly, not wishing Tony to hear that he had been inquiring after him.

CHAPTER XXII.

RUDOLPH FINDS TONY.

RUDOLPH was very much elated at what he had heard. His object then was already attained, and the boy was found.

"Well, good luck has come to me at last," he said to himself. "The young scoundrel is found, and now I must consider how to get him into my hands once more."

The Quaker, to designate him according to his present appearance, at once made his way back to the hotel. He wanted to see Tony and verify the information he had obtained from the boys, though he saw no reason to doubt it.

"There can't be two Tony Rugg's in the world," he said to himself. "I am sure this is the boy."

On reaching the hotel he sauntered out into the stable-yard in the rear of the house. His eyes lighted with pleasure, for he at once caught sight of Tony, standing beside James, the hostler.

"There comes old Broadbrim," said James in a low voice. "The barkeeper told me he took two stiff horns of brandy. He's a queer sort of Quaker in my opinion."

Tony gave a curious glance at the disguised tramp, but entertained no suspicion of his not being what he represented. The white hair and costume made it difficult to doubt.

"I never saw a Quaker before," he said.

"Didn't you?"

Meantime Rudolph came nearer. His disguise had been so successful that he felt perfectly safe from discovery.

"Does thee keep many horses?" he asked.

"Yes, sir; we have twelve."

"That is a large number. Yea, verily, it is," said the tramp.

"Well, it is, but we need them all. There's a good deal of carting to do for the hotel, besides Mr. Porter keeps a livery stable. Was you ever this way before?" asked James, thinking he might as well ask a few questions also.

"Nay, verily."

"Where might you be from?"

"From Philadelphia."

"I've heard there's a good many Quakers out that way."

"Yea, verily, my friend, thee is right."

"Are you going away to-morrow morning?"

"Nay, friend, I think I shall tarry a day or two. Is that lad thy son?"

"Tony, he asks if you are my son," said James, laughing. "No, his name is Tony Rugg, while mine is James Woodley."

"Anthony, was thee born in this town?" asked the tramp, boldly defying detection.

"No, sir," answered Tony. "I only came here a few weeks ago."

"Yea, verily," was the only comment Rudolph made.

"I'd like to choke the boy. I can hardly keep my hands off him," he said to himself. "But I'd better be going. He is looking at me closely. He might suspect something."

"Good-night," he said, and the two responded civilly to the salutation.

"Well, Tony, what do you think of Broadbrim?" asked James.

"I don't know, there's something in his voice that sounds familiar to me."

"Perhaps you may have met him somewhere before," suggested the hostler.

"No, I am sure I have not. I never met any Quaker before."

"Well, there's strange likenesses sometimes. Did I ever tell you my adventure out in Maine?"

"No, what was it?"

"I went down East to see a sister of mine that is married down near Augusta. When, as I was goin' through Portland, a woman came up and made a great ado about my deserting her. She took me for her husband, and came near having me arrested for desertion. You see I and her husband was as like as two peas, that's what some of her neighbors said."

"How did you get off?"

"Luckily I had documents in my pocket showing who I was. Besides, my brother-in-law happened to be in the city, and he identified me."

Rudolph sat in the public room of the hotel for a time, and then he went up to his room, partly to be out of the way of possible recognition, partly to think how he could manage to get Tony into his clutches once more, without betraying himself, or exciting any interference.

He had a back room, the window of which looked out upon the stable-yard. He seated himself at this window, and in this position could easily see and hear all that passed there.

Tony and the hostler were lounging about, the latter smoking a clay pipe, their work being done for the day.

"Tony," said the hostler, "I almost forgot to tell you, you're to go to Thornton to-morrow."

"What for?"

"There's a top-buggy Mr. Porter has sold to a man there. You're to take it over, and lead the horse back."

"How far is it?"

"About five miles."

"All right. I'd just as leave go as stay here. Can I find the road easily?"

"There's no trouble about that. It's straight all the way. Part of it runs through the woods—about a mile, I should say."

"Did Mr. Porter say when he wanted me to start?"

"About nine o'clock; by that time you'll be through your chores."

"Well, I'm willing."

Rudolph heard this conversation with no little pleasure.

"It's the very chance I was waiting for," he said ,o himself. "I'll lie in wait for him as he comes back. I can easiiy hide in the woods."

CHAPTER XXIII.

THE NEGLECTED WELL.

RUDOLPH took care to breakfast in good season the next morning. He felt that this day was to make his fortune. The deed which would entitle him to a life support was to be perpetrated on that day. He shuddered a little when he reflected that in order to compass this a life must be sacrificed, and that the life of the boy who had been for years under his guardianship, who had slept at his side, and borne with him the perils and privations of his adventurous career. He was a reckless man, but he had never before shed blood, or at any rate taken the life of a human being. He would have been less than human if the near approach of such a crime had not made him nervous and uncomfortable.

But against this feeling he fought strenuously.

"What's the odds?" he said to himself. "The boy's got to die some time or other, and his dying now will make me comfortable for life. No more hungry tramps for me. I'll settle down and be respectable. Eight hundred dollars a year will relieve me from all care, and I shall only need to enjoy myself after this.

Rudolph must have had strange notions of respectability to think it could be obtained by crime; but in fact his idea was that a man who could live on his own means was from that very power respectable, and there are plenty of persons of a higher social grade who share in this delusion.

At a few minutes after nine Tony set out on his journey. It never occurred to him that the old Quaker in suit of sober drab, who sat on the piazza and saw him depart, was a man who cherished sinister besigns upon him. In fact, he had forgotten all about him, and was intent upon his journey alone. Most boys like to drive, and our friend Tony was no exception to this general rule. He thought it much better than working about the stable-yard.

"Take care of yourself, Tony," said James, the hostler, in a friendly tone.

"Oh, yes, I'll do that," said Tony, little dreaming how necessary the admonition was likely to prove.

"I may as well be starting too," thought Rudolph, and some ten minutes afterward he started at a walk along the road which led to Thornton.

"I'll keep on as far as the woods," he thought, "and then I'll form my plans. The boy must not escape me, for I may never have as good a chance to dispose of him again."

About two miles on began the woods to which reference has already been made. The tramp selected this as probably the best part of the road to accomplish his criminal design.

They extended for nearly a mile on either side of the road, and this was likely to facilitate his purpose.

"I'll explore a little," thought Rudolph. "I shall have plenty of time before the boy comes back."

Some forty rods from the road on the right hand side, the tramp discovered a ruined hut, which had once belonged to a recluse who had for years lived apart from his kind. This had now fallen into decay,for the former occupant had been for some time dead, and no one had been tempted to succeed him.

The general appearance of the building satisfied Rudolph that it was deserted. Impelled partly by curiosity,he explored the neighborhood of the house.

A rod to the east there was a well, open to the view, the curb having decayed, and being in a ruined condition, Rudolph looked down into it, and judged that it might be about twenty feet deep.

A diabolical suggestion came to him. If he could only lure Tony to this well and dispose of him forever."

"I'll do it," he muttered to himself, and started to return to the road, where he hoped to intercept our hero.

Poor Tony! he little dreamed of the danger that menaced him.

CHAPTER XXIV.

THE DEED IS DONE.

Tony drove rapidly to Thornton and sought the purchaser of the buggy. There was a delay of half an hour in finding him, but at last his business was done, and he set out for home.

It was not quite so amusing leading the horse as sitting in a buggy and driving him. But all our pleasures have to be paid for, and Tony was ready to pay the price of this one. After all, he reflected, it was quite as amusing as working about the stable yard, especially after it occurred to him to mount the animal and thus spare himself fatigue.

Everything went smoothly till he entered the woody part of the road.

"Now I shall be home soon," he said to himself. "But, hallo! who's that?" as a figure stepped out from the side of the road. "Oh, it's the Quaker. I wonder what brought him here?"

"Friend, is thee in a hurry?" asked the impostor.

"I suppose I ought to get back as soon as I can," said Tony. "Why, what's up?"

"Thee is the boy from the hotel, is thee not?" asked Rudolph.

"Yes. You're the Quaker gentleman that is stopping there?"

" Yes."

" Well, what do you want of me?"

"There's a man in the woods that has fallen down a well, and I fear he is badly hurt."

"A man fallen down a well!" exclaimed Tony.

"Yes."

" Where is the well?"

" Back in the woods."

" How did you find him?"

"I was walking for amusement when I heard groans, and looking down I could see the poor man."

Tony never thought of doubting this statement, and said, in a tone of genuine sympathy: "Poor fellow!"

" Will thee go with me and help get him out ?" asked the Quaker.

" Yes," said Tony, readily, "I'll do it. Never mind if I am a little late. Where shall I put the horse?"

" Lead him into the woods and tie him to a tree."

" All right. I guess that'll be the best way."

The horse was disposed of as had been suggested, and the two set forth on what Tony supposed to be their charitable errand.

" I don't see what made you go into the woods?" said our hero, a little puzzled.

" I was brought up in the woods, my young friend. It reminds me of the time when I was a boy like thee."

" Oh, that's it. Well, it was lucky for the man,

that is if we can get him out. Did you speak to him?"

"Yes, verily."

"And did he answer?"

"He groaned. I think he was insensible. I saw that I should need help, and I came to the road again. Luckily thee came by."

"Had you been waiting long?"

"Only five minutes," answered Rudolph.

In reality he had been compelled to wait near an hour, much to his disgust. In fact, he had been led to fear that there might be some other road by which one could return from Thornton, and that Tony had taken it. Should this be the case, his elaborate trap would be useless.

They had come quite near the ruined dwelling, and already the curb of the well was visible.

"Is that the well?" asked Tony.

"Yes," answered the Quaker.

"Let us hurry, then," said Tony.

But the time had come when Tony was to have revealed to him the real character of his companion. A branch, which hung unusually low, knocked off the hat and wig of the pseudo Quaker, and Tony was petrified with dismay when he saw revealed the black, cropped head and sinister face of Rudolph, the tramp.

"Rudolph!" he exclaimed, stopping short in his amazement.

"Yes," said the tramp, avowing himself, now that he saw disguise was useless; "it's Rudolph. At last

I have you, you young scamp!" and he seized the boy's arm as in the grip of a vise.

Tony tried to shake off the grip, but what could a boy do against an athletic man.

"It's no use," said the tramp, between his teeth, I've got you, and I don't mean to let you go."

"What do you mean to do, Rudolph?" asked Tony, uneasily.

"What do I mean to do? I mean to make you repent of what you've done to me, you young whelp."

"What have I done?"

"What haven't you done? You've betrayed me, and sold me to my enemies. That's what you've done."

"I've only done what I was obliged to do. I don't want to do you any more harm. Let me go, and I won't meddle with you any more, nor say a word about you at the hotel."

"Really," said Rudolph, with a disagreeable sneer, "I feel very much obliged to you. You are very kind, upon my soul. So you won't tell them at the hotel that the Quaker gentleman is only a tramp after all.

"No, I will say nothing about you."

"I don't think you are to be trusted, boy."

"Did you ever know me to tell a lie, Rudolph?" asked Tony, proudly. "I don't pretend to be a model boy, but there's one thing I won't do, and that is lie."

"I think I had better make sure that you don't

say anything about me," said the tramp, significantly.

"How?" asked Tony.

"I don't mean to let you go back to the hotel at all."

"But I must go back. I must drive the horse back."

"That's of no importance."

"Yes, it is," persisted Tony, anxiously. "They will think I have stolen it."

"Let them think so."

"But I don't want them to think me a thief."

"I can't help it."

"What are you going to do with me? Where are we going?"

"Before I tell you that I will tell you something more. You have often asked me who you were."

"You always told me I was your son."

"It was not true," said Rudolph, calmly. "You are not related to me."

"I felt sure of it."

"Oh, you did!" sneered the tramp. "You are glad that you are not my son!"

"Who am I?"

"I will tell you this much, that you are the heir to a fortune."

"I the heir to a fortune!" exclaimed Tony, in natural excitement.

"Yes; and I could help you to secure it if I pleased."

Tony knew not what to say or to think. Was it

possible that he—Tony, the tramp—was a gentleman's son, and heir to a fortune? It was almost
incredible. Moreover, what was the object of Rudolph in imparting this secret, and at this time,
when he sought revenge upon him.

"Is this true?" he asked.

"Perfectly true."

"And you know my real name and family?"

"Yes, I do."

"Oh, Rudolph, tell me who I am," Tony said,
imploringly. "Help me to the fortune which you say
I am entitled to, and I will take care that you are
rewarded."

Rudolph surveyed the boy, whom he still held in
his firm grasp, and watched his excitement with
malicious satisfaction.

"There is one objection to my doing that, boy," he
said.

"What is that?"

"I'll tell you," he hissed, as his grasp grew tight-
er, and his dark face grew darker yet with passion,
"*I hate you!*"

This he uttered with such intensity that Tony,
brave as he was, was startled and dismayed.

"Then why did you tell me?" he asked.

"That you might know what you are going to
lose—that you might repent betraying me," answered Rudolph, rapidly. "You ask me what I am
going to do with you? I am going to throw you
down that well, and leave you there—to die!"

Then commenced a struggle between the man

and boy. Tony knew what he had to expect, and he fought for dear life. Rudolph found that he had undertaken no light task, but he, too, was desperate. He succeeded at last in dragging Tony to the well-curb, and, raising him in his sinewy arms, he let him fall.

Then, without waiting to look down, he hurried out of the wood with all speed. He reached the hotel, settled his bill, and paid to have himself carried over to the nearest railroad station.

Not until he was fairly seated in the cars, and was rushing through the country at the rate of thirty miles an hour, did he pause to congratulate himself.

"Now for an easy life!" he ejaculated. "My fortune is made! I shall never have to work any more."

CHAPTER XXV.

"I HOLD YOU TO THE BOND."

ON reaching New York, Rudolph made his way at once to the shop from which he had obtained his Quaker dress.

"Has thee come back ?" asked the old man, in a jocular tone.

"Yea, verily," answered Rudolph.

"How do you like being a Quaker ?"

"I've had enough of it. I want you to take them back. You promised to return me twenty-five dollars."

"Let me look at them," said the old man, cautiously.

"They've seen hard usage," he said. "Look at that rip, and that spot."

"Humbug !" answered Rudolph. "There's nothing but what you can set straight in half an hour, and five dollars is handsome pay for that."

But the old man stood out for seven, and finally the tramp, though grumbling much, was obliged to come to his terms.

"Where have you been ?" asked the old man, whose curiosity was aroused as to what prompted Rudolph to obtain the disguise.

"That's my business," said Rudolph, who had his reasons for secrecy, as we know.

"I meant no offense—I only wondered if you left the city."

"Yes, I've been into New Jersey," answered the tramp, who thought it politic to put the customer on the wrong scent. "You see I've got an old uncle—a Quaker—living there. The old man's got plenty of money, and I thought if I could only make him think me a good Quaker, I should stand a good chance of being remembered in his will."

"I see—a capital idea. Did it work?"

"I can't tell yet. He gave me four dollars and his blessing for the present," said Rudolph, carelessly.

"That's a lie every word of it," said the old man to himself, after the tramp went out. "You must try to fix up a more probable story next time, Mr. Rudolph. He's been up to some mischief, probably. However, it's none of my business, I've made seven dollars out of him, and that pays me well—yes, it pays me well."

When Rudolph left the costumer's, it occurred to him that the tramp's dress which he had resumed had better be changed, partly because he thought it probable that a journey lay before him. He sought out a large ready-made clothing establishment on Fulton street, and with the money which had been returned to him obtained a respectable-looking suit, which quite improved his appearance. He regarded his reflection in a long mirror with considerable satisfaction. He felt that he would now be taken for a respectable citizen, and that in discarding his old dress he had removed all vestiges of the tramp. In this, however, he was not wholly right. His face and general expression he could not change. A careful observer could read in them something of the life he had lead. Still he was changed for the better, and it pleased him.

"Now," he reflected, "I had better go and see Mrs. Harvey Middleton. I have done the work, and I shall claim the reward."

He hurried to the St. Nicholas, and, experienced now in the ways of obtaining access to a guest, he wrote his name on a card and sent it up.

"The lady will see you," was the answer brought back by the servant.

"Of course she will," thought Rudolph. "She'll want to know whether it's all settled, and she has no further cause for fear."

Mrs. Middleton looked up as he entered.

"Sit down, Mr. Rugg," she said, politely.

Her manner was cool and composed; but when the servant had left the room, she rose from her chair, and in a tone which showed the anxiety which she had till then repressed, she asked, abruptly: "Well, Mr. Rugg, have you any news for me?"

"Yes, ma'am, I have," he answered, deliberately.

"What is it? Don't keep me in suspense," she said, impatiently.

"The job's done," said Rudolph briefly.

"You mean that the boy—

"Accidentally fell down a well, and was killed," said the visitor, finishing the sentence.

"Horrible!" murmured the lady.

"Wasn't it?" said Rudolph, with a grin. "He must have been very careless."

Mrs. Middleton did not immediately speak. Though she was responsible for this crime, having instigated it, she was really shocked when it was brought home to her.

"You are sure he is dead?" she said, after a pause.

"When a chap pitches head-first down a well thirty feet deep, there isn't much hope for him, is there?"

"No, I suppose not. Where did this accident happen?" asked the lady.

"That ain't important," answered Rudolph. "It's happened—that's all you need to know. Tony won't never come after that estate of his."

"It would have done him little good. He was not fitted by education to assume it."

"No; but he might have been educated. But that's all over now. It's your's. Nobody can take it from you."

"True!" said Mrs. Middleton, and a look of pleasure succeeded the momentary horror. "You will be ready to testify that the boy is dead?"

"There won't be any danger, will there? They won't ask too many questions?"

"As to that, I think we had better decide what we will say. It won't be necessary to say how the boy died."

"Won't it?"

"No. Indeed, it will be better to give a different account."

"Will that do just as well?"

"Yes. You can say, for instance, that he died of small-pox while under your care in St. Louis, or any other place."

"And that I tended him to the last with the affection of a father," added Rudolph, grinning.

"To be sure. You must settle upon all the details of the story, so as not to be caught in any discrepancies."

"What's that?" asked the tramp, rather mystified.

"Your story must hang together. It mustn't contradict itself."

"To be sure. How long are you going to stay in New York?"

"There is no further occasion for my staying here. I shall sail to England in a week."

"Will it be all right about the money?" asked Rudolph, anxiously.

"Certainly."

"How am I to be sure of that?"

"The word of a lady, sir," said Mrs. Middleton, haughtily, "ought to be sufficient for you."

"That's all very well, but suppose you should get tired of paying me the money?"

"Then you could make it very disagreeable for me by telling all you know about the boy. However, there will be no occasion for that. I shall keep my promise. Will you be willing to sail for England next week."

"Do you mean that I am to go with you?"

"I mean that you are to go. Your testimony must be given on the other side, in order to make clear my title to the estate."

"I see, ma'am. If I'd known that I wouldn't have had no fears about the money."

"You need have none, Mr. Rugg," said Mrs. Middleton, coldly. "The fact is, we are necessary to each other. Each can promote the interests of the other."

"That's so, ma'am. Let's shake hands on that," said Rudolph, advancing with outstretched hand.

"No, thank you," said Mrs. Middleton, coldly. "You forget yourself, sir. Do not forget that I am a lady, and that you are—"

"We are equal, ma'am in this matter," said Rudolph, offended. "You needn't shrink from shaking hands with me."

"That is not in the agreement," said Mrs. Middleton, haughtily. "I shall do what I have agreed, but except so far as it is necessary in the way of business, I wish you to keep yourself away from me. We belong to different grades in society."

"Why didn't you say that the other day, ma'am?" said Rudolph, frowning.

"Because I didn't suppose it to be necessary. You did not offer to shake hands with me then. Besides, at that time you had not—"

"Pushed the boy down the well, if that's what you mean," said Rudolph, bluntly.

"Hush! don't refer to that. I advise you this for your own sake."

"And for the sake of somebody else."

"Mr. Rugg, all this discussion is idle. It can do no good. For whatever service you have rendered, you shall be well paid. That you understand. But it is best that we should know as little of each other henceforth as possible. It might excite suspicion, as you can understand."

"Perhaps you are right, ma'am," said Rudolph, slowly.

"Call here day after to-morrow, and I will let you know by what steamer I take passage for England, that you may obtain a ticket. Good afternoon."

Rudolph left the lady's presence not wholly pleased.

"Why wouldn't she shake my hand?" he muttered to himself. "She's as deep in it as I am."

CHAPTER XXVI.

TONY'S ESCAPE.

WE must now return to our young hero, who was certainly in a critical position. Though strong of his age, the reader will hardly be surprised that he should have been overpowered by a man like Rudolph.

When the false Quaker's hat and wig were taken off, though he was at first surprised, he for the first time understood why the man's face and voice had seemed familiar to him from the time they first met.

He struggled in vain against the fate in store for him. He felt that with him it was to be a matter of life and death, and taken by surprise though he was, he was on the alert to save his life if he could.

The well curb was partially destroyed, as we have said, but the rope still hung from it. At the instant of his fall, Tony managed while in transit to grasp the rope by one hand. He swung violently from one side to the other, and slipped a few feet downward. This Rudolph did not see, for as soon as he had hurled the boy into the well he hurried away.

Tony waited for the rope to become steady before attempting to ascend hand over hand. Unfortunately for his purpose the rope was rotten, and broke just above where he grasped it, precipitating him to

the bottom of the well. But he was already so far
from the opening that his fall was not over ten feet.
Luckily also the water was not over two feet in
depth. Therefore, though he was jarred and startled by the sudden descent, he was not injured.

" Well," thought Tony, " I'm as low as I can get
—that's one comfort. Now is there any chance of
my getting out? "

He looked up, and it gave him a peculiar sensation to look up at the blue sky from the place where
he stood. He feared that Rudolph was still at hand
and would resist any efforts he might make to get
out of the well.

" If he don't interfere I'm bound to get out," he
said to himself, pluckily.

His feet were wet, of course, and this was far
from comfortable.

He made a brief examination of the situation,
and then decided upon his plan. The well, like
most in the country, was provided by a wall of
stones, piled one upon another. In parts it looked
rather loose, and Tony shuddered as he thought of
the possibility of the walls falling, and his being
buried in the ruins.

"It would be all up with me, then," he thought,
" I must get out of this as soon as I can. If I can
only climb up as far as the rope I can escape."

This, in fact, seemed to be his only chance. Using
the wall as a ladder, he began cautiously to ascend.
More than once he came near falling a second time,
but by greatest exertion he finally reached the rope.

He did not dare to trust to it entirely, but contrived to ascend as before, clinging to the rope with his hands. He was in constant fear that it would break a second time, but the strain upon it was not so great, and finally, much to his delight, he reached the top.

He breathed a deep sigh of relief when he found himself once more on *terra firma*. He looked about him cautiously, under the apprehension that Rudolph might be near by, and ready to attack him again. But, as we know, his fears were groundless.

"He made sure that I was disposed of," thought Tony. "What could have induced him to attempt my life? Can it be true, as he said, that I am heir to a fortune? Why couldn't he tell me? I would have paid him well for the information when I got my money. Then he said he knew who I was—I care more for that than the money."

But Tony could not dwell upon these thoughts. The claims of duty were paramount. He must seek the horse, and go back to the hotel. He had been detained already for nearly three-quarters of an hour, and they would be wondering what had become of him.

He made his way as quickly as possible to where he had tied the horse. But he looked for him in vain. He had been untied and led away—perhaps stolen. Tony felt assured that the horse of himself could not leave the spot.

"It must be Rudolph," he said to himself. "He

has made off with the horse. Now I am in trouble. What will Mr. Porter say to me?"

Tony was in error, as we know, in concluding that Rudolph had carried away the horse. The tramp had no use for him. Besides, he knew that such a proceeding would have exposed him to suspicion, which it was very important for him to avoid.

Who, then, had taken the horse? That is a question which we are able to answer, though Tony could not.

Fifteen minutes before Sam Payson, whose place Tom had taken, with a companion, Ben Hardy, while wandering through the woods had espied a horse.

"Hallo!" said Ben, "here's a horse."

"So it is," said Sam. "It's rather odd that he should be tied here."

"I wonder whose it is?"

Sam had been examining him carefully, and had recognized him.

"It's Mr. Porter's Bill. Don't you see that white spot? That's the way I know him. I have harnessed that horse fifty times."

"But how did he come here? That's the question?"

"I'll tell you," said Sam. "I was at the hotel this morning, and heard that that boy Tony was to go over to Thornton with him."

"That don't explain why he is tied here, does it?"

"Tony must have tied him while he was taking a

tramp in the woods. Wouldn't Porter be mad if he knew it?"

"I shouldn't wonder if Tony would get bounced."

"Nor I. I tell you what, Ben, I've a great mind to untie the horse, and take him back myself."

"What's the good? It would be an awful job. We came out here to have some fun," grumbled Ben.

"This would be fun to me. I'll get Tony into trouble, and very likely get back the place he cheated me out of. I guess it'll pay."

"All right, Sam. I didn't think of that. I'd like to see how Tony looks when he comes back, and finds the horse gone."

"It'll serve him right," said Sam. "What business had he to interfere with me, I'd like to know."

"If you're going to do it you'd better hurry up. He may go back any time."

"That's so. Here goes, then."

In a trice Bill was untied, and Sam taking the halter led him away. When Tony came up he was not in sight.

Though Tony felt convinced that Rudolph had carried away the horse, he felt it to be his duty to look about for it. There was a bare chance that he might find it somewhere in the wood. In this way he lost considerable time. Had he started for the hotel immediately he would very likely have overtaken the two boys.

Sam kept on his way, and finally arrived at the hotel.

As he led the horse into the stable-yard James,
the hostler, exclaimed in surprise:

"How came you by that horse, Sam Payson?"

"Is that the way you thank me for bringing him
back?" asked Sam.

"He left the stable under the charge of Tony Rugg
this morning."

"Pretty care he takes of him, then."

"What do you mean? Where did you find him?"

"Down in the woods."

"What woods?"

"Between here and Thornton."

"Wasn't Tony with him?"

"No."

"Are you sure of that? Are you sure you two
boys didn't attack Tony and take the horse away?"
demanded James, suspiciously.

"No, we didn't. If you don't believe me, you
may ask Ben."

"How was it, Ben?" he asked.

"Just as Sam has said. We found the horse alone
in the woods. We thought he might be stolen, and
we brought him home. It was a good deal of trouble, for it's full two miles."

James looked from one to the other in perplexity.

"I don't understand it at all," he said. "It don't
look like Tony to neglect his duty that way."

"You've got too high an opinion of that boy entirely," said Sam, sneeringly.

Tony sprung forward and seized the would-be murderer by the arm.
(See page 182.)

CHAPTER XXVII.

TONY IS DISCHARGED.

Presently Tony came into the yard. He was looking very sober. He had lost the horse, and he didn't know how to excuse himself. He didn't feel that he had been to blame, but he suspected that he should be blamed nevertheless.

"What did you do with the horse, Tony?" asked James.

"He was stolen from me," answered Tony.

"How could that be?"

"I expect it was the Quaker."

"The Quaker!" repeated James, in amazement. "Are you sure you're not crazy—or drunk?"

"Neither one," said Tony. "It's a long story and——"

"You must tell it to Mr. Porter then. He wants to see you right off. But I'll tell you for your information that the horse is here."

"Is here? Who brought it?"

"Sam Payson brought it a short time since."

"Sam Payson! Where did he say he found it?"

"In the woods."

"Then he might have left it there," said Tony, indignantly. "What business had he to untie it, and give me all this trouble?"

"You can speak to Mr. Porter about that."

"Where is he?"

"In the office."

Tony entered the office.

Mr. Porter regarded him with a frown.

"How is this, Tony?" he began. "You leave my horse in the woods to be brought home by another boy. He might have been stolen, do you know that?"

"I've been deceived, aud led into a trap," said Tony.

"What on earth do you mean? Who has deceived and trapped you?"

"The Quaker who was stopping here. Has he come back?"

"He has settled his bill and left the hotel. What cock-and-bull story is this you have hatched up?"

"It is a true story, Mr. Porter. This man was not a Quaker at all. He was a tramp."

"Take care what you say, Tony. Do you take me for a fool?"

"He is a man I used to know. When I was coming home he was waiting for me in the woods, only I didn't know who he really was. He told me there was a man who had fallen into a well in the woods, and he wanted my help to get him out. So I tied the horse and went with him. I wouldn't have left him but for the story of the man in the well."

"Go on," said the landlord. "I warn you I don't believe a word of this wonderful story of yours."

"I can't help it," said Tony, desperately. It's true."

"Go on, and I'll give you my opinion of it afterward."

"Just before we got to the well a branch took off his hat and wig, and I saw that he was no Quaker, but my enemy, Rudolph Rugg."

"Rudolph Rugg! A very good name for a romance."

Tony proceeded:

"Then I tried to get away, but it was too late. The man seized me and threw me down the well. But first he told me that he knew who I was, and that I was heir to a large fortune."

"Indeed! How happens it that you are not at the bottom of the well still?"

"I got out."

"So I see; but how?"

"I climbed up by the stones till I reached the rope, and then I found it easy. I hurried to where I had left the horse, but it was gone. I supposed that the Quaker had taken it, but James tells me Sam Payson found it and brought it back."

"Look here, boy," said the landlord, sternly, "do you expect me to believe this romance of yours?"

"I don't know whether you will or not, sir. All I can say is that it is the exact truth."

"I cannot keep you in my employ any longer. I have been deceived by you, and should no longer trust you. You certainly have mistaken your vocation. You are not fit to be a stable boy."

"I should like to know what I am fit for," said Tony, despondently.

"I will tell you, then. Judging from the story you have told me, I should think you might succeed very well in writing a romance. I don't know whether it pays, but you can try it."

"Some time you will find out that I have told the truth," said Tony.

"Perhaps so, but I doubt it."

"When do you want me to go?"

"You can stay till to-morrow morning. Wait a minute. Here is a five-dollar bill. That is a fair price for the time you have been with me."

As Tony was going out he came near having a collision with Sam Payson.

Sam looked at him inquiringly.

"Have you been discharged?" he asked.

"Yes," said Tony. "It was your fault. What made you take that horse?"

"I was afraid Mr. Porter might lose it. Is he in?"

"Yes. You can apply for my place, if you want to."

"I mean to."

Sam went in, and addressed the landlord.

"I brought your horse back," he said.

"Thank you. Here's two dollars for your trouble."

Sam tucked it away with an air of satisfaction.

"Tony tells me he is going away."

"Yes. He don't suit me."

"Wouldn't I suit you?" asked Sam, in an ingratiating tone.

"No; I've tried you, and you won't suit," was the unexpected reply.

"But I brought back the horse," pleaded Sam, crest-fallen.

"I've paid you for that," said the landlord. "Didn't I pay you enough?"

"Yes, sir; but I thought you'd take me back again."

"I know you too well, Sam Payson, to try any such experiment. The Widow Clark told me yesterday that she wanted to get her boy into a place, and I am going to offer it to him.

"He don't know anything about horses," said Sam.

"He will soon learn. He is a good boy, and industrious. I am sure he will suit me better than you."

"I wish I hadn't brought back his old horse,' muttered Sam, as he left the office and went back into the yard. He hoped to triumph over Tony by telling him that he had taken his place, but the opportunity was not allowed him.

"Well, Sam, are you going to take my place?" asked Tony.

"No, I'm not," said Sam.

"Didn't you ask for it?"

"The old man had promised it to another boy," said Sam, sourly.

"He's been pretty quick about it, then," said James.

"A boy that don't know the first thing about horses," grumbled Sam.

"Who is it?"

"Joe Clark."

"He's a good boy; I'm glad he's coming, though I'm sorry to lose Tony."

"Thank you, James," said Tony. "I'd like to stay, but I can't blame Mr. Porter for not believing my story. It was a strange one, but it's true for all that."

James shrugged his shoulders.

"Then you believe you're heir to a fortune, as he told you?"

"Yes; he had no reason to tell me a lie."

"What's that?" asked Sam.

"The Quaker gentleman who was here told Tony that he was heir to a large fortune."

"Ho, ho!" laughed Sam, boisterously. "That's a likely story, that is."

"Why isn't it?" asked Tony, frowning.

"You heir to a fortune—a clodhopper like you! Oh! I shall split!" said Sam, giving way to another burst of merriment.

"I am no more a clodhopper than you are," said Tony, "and I advise you not to laugh too much, or I may make you laugh on the other side of your mouth."

"It'll take more than you to do it," said Sam, defiantly,

"I have done it already, Sam Payson, and I'm ready to try it again before I leave town."

"I wouldn't dirty my hands with you," said Sam, scornfully.

"You'd better not."

When Sam had gone, Tony turned to James.

"I wonder whether I shall ever see you again, James?" he said, thoughtfully.

"I hope so, Tony. I'm sorry you're going; but you couldn't expect Mr. Porter to believe such a story as that."

"Then you don't believe it, James? I'll come back some day just to prove to you that it is true."

"Come back at any rate; I shall be glad to see you. When do you go?"

"To-morrow morning."

"Where shall you go first?"

"To New York; but I'll help you till I go."

So Tony did his work as usual for the remainder of the day. He felt rather sober. Just as he had found a home his evil genius, in the character of Rudolph, appeared and deprived him of it.

CHAPTER XXVIII.

THE WORLD BEFORE HIM.

THOUGH Tony was out of a place he was considerably better off than he had generally been. He had five dollars in his pocket for the first time in his life. A few weeks ago he would have considered himself rich with this amount, and would have been in high spirits. But now he took a different view of life. He had known what it was to have a settled home, and to earn an honest living, and he had learned to like it. But fortune was against him, and he must go.

"Good-by, James," he said, soberly, to the hostler the next morning.

"Good-by, Tony, and good luck," said the kind-hearted hostler.

"I hope I shall have good luck, but I don't expect it," said Tony.

"Pooh, nonsense ! You're young, and the world is before you."

"That's so, James, but so far the world has been against me."

"Come here a minute, Tony," said James, lowering his voice.

As Tony approached, he thrust a bank-note hastily into his hand.

"Take it," he said, quickly. "I don't need it, and you may."

Tony looked at the bill, and found it was a ten-dollar note.

"You're very kind, James," he said, touched by a kindness to which he was unaccustomed, "but I can't take it."

"Why not? I shan't need it."

"Nor I, James. I've got some money. It isn't much, but I'm used to roughing it. I've done it all my life. I always come down on my feet like a cat."

"But you may get hard up."

"If I do, I'll let you know."

"Will you promise that?"

"Honor bright."

So James took back the money reluctantly, and Tony bade him good-by.

It was a rainy day when Tony arrived in New York. The stores were deserted, and the clerks lounged idly behind the counter. Only those who were actually obliged to be out appeared in the streets. If Tony's hopes had been high they would have been lowered by the dreary weather. He wandered aimlessly about the streets, having no care about his luggage for he had brought none, looking about him listlessly. He found himself after a while in the lower part of Broadway, not far from the Battery. It is here, as my city readers know, the most of the European steamer lines have their offices.

At once Tony saw a figure that attracted his eager attention.

It was Rudolph Rugg, his old comrade, and now bitter enemy.

"Where is he going?" thought Tony.

This question was soon solved.

Rudolph entered the office of the Anchor Line of steamers.

"What can he want there?" thought Tony. "I'll watch him."

He took a position near by, yet far enough off to avoid discovery, and waited patiently for Rudolph to reappear. He waited about fifteen minutes. Then he saw the tramp come out with a paper in his hand, which he appeared to regard with satisfaction. He turned and went up Broadway.

As soon as he thought it safe Tony crossed the street and entered the office. He made his way up to the counter and inquired the price of passage. The rates were given him.

"Can you tell me," he asked, carelessly, "if a Mr. Rugg is going across on one of your steamers?"

"Mr. Rugg? Why, it is the man who just left the office."

"Did he buy a passage ticket?"

"Yes."

"When does he sail?"

"On Saturday."

"And where does he go?"

"To Liverpool, of course. Can I sell you a ticket?"

"I haven't decided," said Tony.

"If you go, you will find it to your advantage to go by our line."

"I'll go by your line, if I go at all," said Tony. "I wonder whether he'd be so polite if he knew I had but three dollars and a quarter in my pocket?" said our hero to himself.

Then he began to wonder how it happened that Rudolph was going. First, it was a mystery where he could have obtained the money necessary for the purchase of a ticket. Next, what could be his reason for leaving America.

"Probably he has picked somebody's pocket," thought Tony.

That disposed of the difficulty, but, as we know, Tony was mistaken. It was money that he had received for a worse deed, but Tony never thought of connecting the state of Rudolph's purse with the attempt that had been made upon his own life.

When Tony came to think of it he felt glad that Rudolph was going abroad. He felt that his own life would be safer with an ocean flowing between him and the man who latterly had exhibited such an intense hatred for him. As to his motive, why perhaps he thought that he would be safer in London than in New York.

Tony bethought himself of securing a temporary home. He was not a stranger in New York, and knew exactly where to go. There was a house not far from Greenwich street, where he had lodged more than once before, and where he was known. It was far from a fashionable place, but the charge was small, and that was a necessary consideration with Tony.

He rang the bell, and the proprietor, a hard-favored woman of fifty, came to open it.

"How do you do, Mrs. Blodgett?" said Tony.

"Why, it's Tony," said the woman, not unkindly, "Where have you been this long time?"

"In the country." answered our hero.

"And where is your father?"

"Do you mean the man I used to be with?"

"Yes. He was your father, wasn't he?"

"No. He was no relation of mine," said Tony, hastily. "We used to go together, that is all."

"Where is he?"

"I don't know exactly. We had a falling out, and we've parted."

"Well, Tony, what can I do for you?"

"Have you got any cheap room to let, Mrs. Blodgett?"

"I've got a room in the attic. It's small, but if it'll suit you, you can have it for a dollar a week."

"It's just the thing," said Tony, in a tone of satisfaction. "Can I go right up?"

"Yes, if you want to. I generally want a week's pay in advance, but you've been here before ——"

"No matter for that. Here's the money," said Tony.

"I'll show you the way up."

"All right. I guess I'll lie down awhile. I've been about the streets all day, and am pretty tired."

The room was quite small, and the furniture was shabby and well-worn ; but Tony was not particu lar. He threw himself on the bed, and soon fell asleep.

How long he slept he did not know, but when he woke up the room was quite dark. He stretched, and did not immediately remember where he was ; but it flashed upon him directly.

"I wonder what time it is ?" he asked himself. "I must have slept a long time. I feel as fresh as a lark. I'll get up a take and tramp."

When he went down stairs he found that it was already ten o'clock.

"I feel as fresh as if it were morning," thought Tony. "I'll go out on Broadway and watch some of the theatres when the people come out."

Ten o'clock seems late in the country ; it is the usual hour for retiring for many families ; but in the city it is quite different. There are still many to be seen in the streets, and for many it is the com- mencement of a season of festivity.

Tony walked for half an hour. He was so thor- oughly rested that he felt no fatigue. Presently he stepped into a crowded billiard-room, and seating himself, began to watch a game between a young man of twenty-five and a man probably fifteen years his senior. The first was evidently a gentle- man by birth and education ; his dress and manners evinced this. The other looked like an adventurer, though he was well-dressed.

"Come, let us play for drinks," said the elder.

"I've drank enough," said the young man.

"Nonsense. You can stand a little more."

"Just as you say."

The game terminated in favor of the elder, and the drinks were brought.

This went on for some time. The young man was evidently affected. Finally he threw down his cue, and said;

"I won't play again."

"Why not?"

"My hand is unsteady. I have drank too much."

"I've drank as much as you, but I am all right."

"You can stand more than I. I'll settle for the drinks and games and go home."

"Shan't I see you home?" asked the elder.

"I don't want to trouble you."

"No trouble at all."

The young man paid at the bar, displaying a well-filled pocketbook. There was something in his companion's expression which made Tony suspicious. He formed a sudden resolve.

"I'll follow them," he said, and when they left the room he was close behind them.

CHAPTER XXIX.

A STRANGE ADVENTURE.

THE young man leaned on the arm of his companion. He was affected by the potations in which he had indulged, and was sensible of his condition.

"I ought not to have drank so much," he said, in unsteady accents.

"Pooh! it's nothing," said the other, lightly. "Where are you stopping?"

"St. Nicholas."

"We'd better walk; it will do you good to walk.'

"Just as you say."

"Of course, I would only advise you for your good."

"I know it; but old fellow, why did you make me drink so much?"

"I thought you could stand it better. I'm as cool as a cucumber."

He pressed the young man's arm, and led him into a side street.

"What's that for? This ain't the way to St. Nicholas."

"I know it."

"Why don't you go up Broadway?"

"You are not fit to go in yet. You need a longer walk, so that your condition will not be noticed when you go in."

"Go along old fellow; you're right."

Still Tony kept behind. All seemed right enough, but somehow he could not help feeling suspicious of the older man.

"I'll watch him," he thought, "and if he attempts any mischief I'll interfere."

The two men walked in a westerly direction, crossing several streets.

"Look here," said the young man, "we'd better turn back."

Now was the time.

The other looked swiftly around, but did not notice Tony, who was tracking him in the darkness.

"Give me your watch and money at once, or I'll blow your brains out."

"Look here, you're only trying to play a joke on me."

"You're mistaken. I'm a desperate man. I will do as I say."

"Then you're a villian," said the young man, with spirit. "You've made me drunk in order to rob me."

"Precisely. Your money or your life. That's about what I mean."

"I'll call the police."

"If you do it will be your last word. Now make up your mind."

The young man, instead of complying, endeavored to break away, but in his intoxication he had lost half his strength, and was no match for the other.

"You fool! your blood be on your own hands!" said his companion, and he drew a pistol from his side pocket.

An instant and he would have fired, but Tony was on the alert. He sprang forward, seized the would-be murderer by the arm, and the pistol went off, but the bullet struck a brick wall on the opposite side of the street.

"Police!" shouted Tony, at the top of his lungs.

"Confusion!" exclaimed the villian. "I must be getting out of this."

He turned to fly, but Tony seized him by the coat, and he struggled fiercely, but iu vain.

"Let go, you young scoundrel!" he shouted, "or I'll shoot you."

"With an unloaded pistol?" asked Tony. "That don't scare much."

A quick step was heard, and a policeman turned the corner.

"What's the matter?" he asked.

"I charge this man with an attempt at murder," said Tony.

"The boy is right," said the young man.

"They are both lying," said the adventurer, furiously. "It's a plot against me."

"I know you, Bill Jones," said the policeman, after a careful scrutiny of the man's features. "You're a hard ticket. Come along with me. You two must go with me to prefer your charge."

"Let me have your arm, my boy," said the young man; "I'm ashamed to own that I need your help. It is the last time I will allow liquor to get the better of me."

"I guess you're about right there," said Tony. "You've had a narrow escape."

"I owe my life to you," said the young man, warmly. "How did you happen to come up just in the nick of time?"

"I suspected the man meant you no good. I followed you from the billiard saloon, where I saw you playing."

"You were sharper than I. I never suspected harm. You have done me the greatest possible service."

"Curse the young brat!" muttered the man in custody. "I'd like a good chance to wring your neck."

"I've no doubt of it," said Tony. "I'll keep out of your way."

The station house was not far off. The party entered. The charge was formally made, and Tony and the young man went out.

"Won't your father and mother feel anxious about your being out so late?" asked George Spencer, for this was the young man's name.

"I don't think they will," answered Tony. "I haven't got any for that matter."

"Who do you live with then?"

"I take care of myself."

"Have you no one belonging to you?"

"Not one."

"Are you poor?" asked Spencer, for the first time taking notice of Tony's rather shabby apparel.

"Oh, no," said our hero. "I've got a little over two dollars in my pocket."

"Is that all?"

"Yes, and it's a good deal more than I generally have."

"You don't say so. How do you make your living?"

"Any way I can. Any way that's honest."

"And don't you ever get discouraged—down in the mouth?"

"Not often," answered Tony. "I've always got along, and I guess something will turn up for me. But there's one thing I'm sorry for."

"What's that?"

"I would like to get some sort of an education; I don't know much."

"Can you read?"

"A little, and write a little. I mostly picked it up myself."

The young man whistled.

"Have you any place to sleep to-night?"

"I've hired an attic room for a week."

"What do you pay?"

"A dollar a week."

"Of course, it's a poor room?"

"Yes; but it's all I can expect, and better than I often have. Why, I've slept in barns and under haystacks plenty of times."

"What is your name?"

"Tony Rugg."

"Well, Tony, you must come and stop with me to-night."

"With you?"

"Yes; at the St. Nicholas Hotel. You can help me get there, and share my room."

Tony hesitated.

"Do you mean it?" he asked.

"Why shouldn't I?"

"Because you're a gentleman, and I—do you know what they call me?"

"What?"

"Tony, the Tramp."

"It is your misfortune and not your fault. I repeat my invitation—will you come?"

"I will," answered Tony.

He saw that the young man was in earnest, and he no longer persisted in his refusal.

"To-morrow morning I will talk with you further about your affairs. I want to do something for you."

"You are very kind."

"I ought to be. Haven't you saved my life? But there is the hotel."

Tony and his new friend entered the great hotel. It was brilliantly lighted, though it was now nearly midnight.

Mr. Spencer went up to the desk.

"My key," he said; "No. 169."

"Here it is, sir."

"This young man will share my room; I will enter his name."

The clerk looked at Tony in surprise. He looked rather shabby for a guest of the great caravansery.

"Has he luggage?" asked the clerk.

"None to night; I will pay his bill."

"All right, sir."

They got into the elevator, and presently came to a stop. Mr. Spencer opened the door of 169.

It was a good-sized and handsomely furnished chamber, containing two beds.

"You will sleep in that bed, Tony," said Spencer. "I feel dead tired. Will you help me off with my coat?"

Scarcely was the young man in bed than he fell asleep. Tony lay awake some time, thinking of his strange adventure.

"It's the first time in my life," he said to himself, "when I've had two beds—one here and the other at my lodgings. What would Rudolph say if he knew I was stopping at a fashionable hotel, instead of being at the bottom of the well, where he threw me?"

CHAPTER XXX.

BREAKFAST AT THE ST. NICHOLAS.

WHEN Tony woke up in the morning he looked about him with momentary bewilderment, wondering where he was.

George Spencer was already awake.

"How did you sleep, Tony?" he asked.

"First rate."

"It must be late. Please look at my watch and tell me what time it is."

"Half-past eight," said Tony, complying with his request. "Why, it's late."

"Not very. I didn't get up until ten yesterday. Well, what do you say to getting up and having some breakfast?"

"Am I to breakfast with you, Mr. Spencer?"

"To be sure you are, unless you have another engagement," added Spencer, jocosely.

"If I have it can wait," said Tony. "How much do they charge here for board, Mr. Spencer?"

"Four or five dollars a day. I really don't know exactly how much."

"Four or five dollars a day!" exclaimed Tony, opening his eyes in amazement. "How much I shall cost you!"

"I expect you will cost me a good deal, Tony,"

said the young man. "Do you know, I have a great
mind to adopt you!"

"Do you really mean it, Mr. Spencer?"

"Yes; why shouldn't I. I like what I have seen
of you, and I have plenty of money."

"It must be a nice thing to have plenty of money," said Tony, thoughtfully.

"There is danger in it, too, Tony. I am ashamed
to tell you how much I have spent in gambling and
dissipation."

"I wouldn't do it, Mr. Spencer," said Toney, soberly.

"Capital advice, Tony. I am going to keep you
with me for fear I might forget, that is, if you think
you will like me well enough to stay."

"I am sure to like you, Mr. Spencer, but you may
get tired of me."

"I'll let you know when I do, Tony. How much
income do you think I have?"

"A thousand dollars!" guessed Tony, who considered that this would be a very large income.

Spencer laughed.

"It is over ten thousand," he said.

"Ten thousand!" exclaimed Tony. "How can
you spend it all?"

"I did spend it all, last year, Tony. and got a
thousand dollars in debt. I gambled, and most of
it went that way. But I'll leave that off. I shall
have you to take up my time, now."

"Did you know that man you played billiards
with last night, Mr. Spencer?"

"I made his acquaintance in a gambling house, and I was well punished for keeping company with such a man."

Tony was now nearly dressed.

"You didn't get your clothing from a fashionable tailor, I should judge," said his new guardian.

"No," said Tony, "I haven't been to fashionable tailors much."

"After breakfast I must go with you and see you properly clothed. If you are to be my ward, I must have your appearance do me credit."

"How very kind you are to me, Mr. Spencer," said Tony, gratefully. "I don't know how to repay you."

"You've done something in that way already."

"It seems like a dream that a poor boy like me should be adopted by a rich gentleman."

"It is a dream you won't wake up from very soon. Now if you are ready we will go down to breakfast."

Tony hung back.

"Won't you be ashamed to have me seen with you in these clothes?" he asked.

"Not a bit. Besides you will soon be in better trim. Come along, Tony."

They went down together, and entered the breakfast room. A considerable number of persons were there. Several stared in surprise at Tony as he entered and took his seat. Our hero noticed it, and it made him nervous.

"Do you see how they look at me?" he said.

"Don't let it affect your appetite, Tony," said his

friend. "When you appear among them again you will have no reason to feel ashamed."

A speech which Tony heard from a neighboring table did not serve to reassure him.

An over-dressed lady of fifty said to a tall, angular young lady, her daughter:

"Elvira, do you see that very common-looking boy at the next table?"

"Yes, ma."

"He looks low. He is not as well dressed as our servants. It is very strange they should let him eat at an aristocratic hotel like this."

"Isn't he with that gentleman, ma?"

"It looks like it. He may be the gentleman's servant. I really think it an imposition to bring him here."

Mr. Spencer smiled.

"Don't mind it, Tony," he said. "I know those people by sight. They are parvenus. I suppose you don't understand the word. They are vulgar people who have become rich by a lucky speculation. They will change their tune presently. What will you have for breakfast?"

"There's such a lot of things," said Tony, "I don't know what to choose."

"You'll get used to that. I'll order breakfast for both."

The waiter appeared, and Mr. Spencer gave the order.

The waiter looked uncomfortable.

"Mr. Spencer," he said, "it's against the rules for you to bring your servant to the table with you."

"I have not done so," said Mr. Spencer, promptly. "This young gentleman is my ward."

"Oh, excuse me," said the waiter, confused.

"Has any one prompted you to speak to me about him?"

"Those ladies at the next table."

"Then those ladies owe an apology to my ward," said the young man, loud enough for the ladies to hear.

The shot told. The ladies looked confused and embarrassed, and Tony and his guardian quietly finished their breakfast.

There was another lady who noticed Tony, and this was Mrs. Harvey Middleton. She was to sail for England in the afternoon.

As Tony and Mr. Spencer were going out of the breakfast-room, they met her entering.

She started at the sight of Tony, and scanned his face eagerly.

"Who are you, boy?" she asked, quickly, laying her hand on his arm.

Tony was too surprised to answer, and Mr. Spencer answered for him.

"It is my ward, madame," he answered. "He has been roughing it in the country, which accounts for the state of his wardrobe."

"O, I beg pardon, sir," said Mrs. Middleton. "I thought his face looked familiar."

"You see, Tony, that your appearance attracts attention," said Mr. Spencer, laughing. "Now we'll go out, and I'll get you a fit-out."

They went to a well-known clothier's, and Mr. Spencer purchased two handsome suits for our hero, one of which he put on at once. At another place a plentiful supply of under-clothing was purchased. Next a hat and shoes were procured. Tony's hair was cut, he took a bath, and in a couple of hours he was transformed into a young gentleman of distinguished appearance.

"Really, Tony, I shouldn't have known you," said his friend.

"I shouldn't have known myself," said Tony. "I almost think it must be some other boy. Who'd think I was Tony, the Tramp, now?"

"You are not to be a tramp any longer, I have not yet formed my plans for you, but I shall soon. I suppose, Tony, your education has been neglected."

"I should think it had," answered Tony. "I'm as ignorant as a horse."

"Then you ought to learn something."

"I wish I could."

"You shall, but, as I said, I must arrange details later."

*   *   *   *   *   *   *

About this time Rudolph and Mrs. Middleton were conversing, preparatory to starting for the steamer.

"You are sure the boy is dead?" she said.

"Sure? I ought to be. Didn't I see him dead with my own eyes?"

"I saw a boy this morning who looked as I suppose the boy would have looked—of the same age, too."

"Where did you see him?"

"He was with a gentleman, coming out of the breakfast-room as I was entering it."

"It couldn't have been he," said Rudolph, positively. "Even if he were alive, he wouldn't be here. But he's dead. I tell you. There's no doubt of it."

"There are strange resemblances," said the lady. "But, of course, it couldn't have been the boy. Indeed, the gentleman with him told me that it was his ward."

Rudolph laughed.

"Tony wasn't likely to have a gentleman for a guardian," he said.

But Rudolph would have felt less easy in his mind if he had known that the boy whom he supposed dead at the bottom of a well was really in the hotel at that very moment.

CHAPTER XXXI.

TONY AND HIS GUARDIAN SET UP HOUSEKEEPING.

"Now, Tony," said George Spencer, after dinner, "I want to tell you what plans I have formed for you and myself. I have got tired of hotel life, and want a home. I shall seek a couple of handsomely-furnished rooms up town, make it social and pleasant with books and pictures, and we will settle down and enjoy ourselves."

"I am afraid you will get tired of me, Mr. Spencer," said Tony, modestly. "I am too ignorant to be much company for you."

"Ignorance, like poverty, can be remedied," said the young man. "I shall obtain a private tutor for you, and expect you to spend some hours daily in learning." Tony's face brightened up.

"That is just what I would like," he said.

"You would like it better than going to school?"

"Yes, for at school I should be obliged to go into a class with much younger boys."

"While with a tutor you can go on as fast as you please."

"Yes, sir."

"To-night we both need a little recreation. Suppose we go to some place of amusement. Have you ever been to Barnum's?"

"Yes, sir, but I didn't take a reserved seat."

"I suppose not."

"I sat in the upper gallery."

"To-night you shall be fashionable. Have you a pair of kid gloves?"

"The last pair I had is worn out," said Tony, laughing.

"Then you must have another pair. We will get a pair on our way there."

It was already time to start.

At eight o'clock Tony found himself occupying an orchestra chair near the stage, his hands encased in a pair of gloves of faultless fit, and looking enough like a young patrician to pass muster among his fashionable neighbors.

"How does it seem, Tony?" asked Spencer, smiling.

"Tip-top," answered Tony; "but how queer kid gloves feel. I never had a pair on in my life before."

"There are the two ladies who found fault with your appearance at the breakfast table this morning."

"They are loooking at me through an opera-glass."

"Wondering if you can be the same boy. I have no doubt they are puzzled to account for your transformation.

Mr. Spencer was right. The two ladies were at the same moment exchanging remarks about our hero.

" Goodness, Elvira! there is that boy that was at breakfast this morning at the hotel,"

" The boy that was so shabbily dressed, mamma? Where?"

" Just to the left. He isn't shabby now. See how he is decked out. Who would have thought it?"

" It's queer, isn't it?"

" I think we must have been mistaken about him. He looks like a young gentleman now. But why should he have worn such clothes before?"

" I can't tell, I am sure."

" That's a nice-looking young man, Elvira. I wish he would take a fancy to you."

" La! mamma, how you talk," said Elvira, bridling and smiling.

" Depend upon it, Tony, those ladies will be polite to you if they get a chance," said Spencer, laughing.

" It makes a great deal of difference how a boy is dressed," said Tony.

" You are right, Tony. Remember you are fashionable now."

" There's a gentleman in front that I know," said Tony, suddenly.

" Where."

" The man with a partly bald head."

" How do you know him?"

" He was staying two or three days at the country hotel where I was stable boy."

" Do you think he would know you now?"

" May I see?"

" Yes, but don't let him find you out.   It won't
do in society to let it be known that you were ever
a stable-boy."

" All right."

Tony leaned over, and addressing the gentleman,
said:

" Would you be kind enough to lend me your
programme a minute, sir?"

" Certainly," was the reply.   Then, looking at
Tony: " Your face looks very familiar.   Where
have I seen you before?"

" Perhap at the St. Nicholas, sir, said Tony; " I
am stopping there."

" No; I never go to the St. Nicholas.   Bless me!
You're the very image of a boy I have seen somewhere."

" Am I? " said Tony.   " I hope he was good-
looking? " .

" He was; but he was not dressed like you.   In
fact—I remember now—he was employed as stable-
boy in a country hotel."

" A stable boy! " exclaimed Tony, with comic
horror.   " I hope you don't think I am the boy."

" Of course not.   But really the resemblance is
striking."

" Mr. Spencer," said Tony, " this gentleman has
met a stable boy who looks like me."

" I really beg your pardon," said the gentleman;
" I meant no offense."

" My ward would not think of taking offense,"
said Mr. Spencer, courteously.

Tony smiled to himself; he had a strong sense of humor, and was much amused.

It is needless to say that he enjoyed the performance—all the more so from his luxurious seat and nearness to the stage.

"Its a good deal better than sitting in the gallery," he said, in a whisper to his companion.

"I should think so. I never sat up there, Tony."

"And I never sat anywhere else."

As they were leaving the house, they found themselves close to the ladies whom they had noticed at breakfast.

Elvira chanced to drop her handkerchief, probably intentionally.

Tony stooped and picked it up. Though he had led the life of a tramp, he had the instincts of a gentleman.

"Thank you, young gentleman," said Elvira. "You are very polite."

"Oh, don't mention it," said Tony.

"Really, Mamma, he is a born gentleman," said Elvira, later, to her mother. "How could we make such a mistake."

"His clothes were certainly very shabby, my dear."

"Very likely he had been out hunting or something. We must not judge so hastily next time."

The ladies were foiled in their intentions of cultivating the acquaintance of Tony and his guardian, as two days later they left the hotel, and installed themselves in an elegant boarding-house on Madison avenue.

"Now," said Mr. Spencer, "we must go to work."

"I must," said Tony.

"And I too," said Spencer.

"What can you have to do?"

"I have received a proposal to invest a part of my money—only one-fourth—in a business down town, and shall accept. I don't need to increase my income, but I think I shall be less likely to yield to temptation if I have some fixed employment. I shall be so situated that I can do as much or as little as I please. As to yourself I have put an advertisement in a morning paper for a teacher, and expect some applicants this morning. I want you to choose for yourself."

"I am afraid I shan't be a very good judge of teachers. Shall I examine them to see if they know enough?"

"I think, from what you say of your ignorance, that any of them will know enough to teach you for the present. The main thing is to select one who knows how to teach, and whom you will like."

"I wish you were a teacher, Mr. Spencer."

"Why?"

"Because then I should have a teacher whom I liked."

"Thank you, Tony," said the young man, evidently gratified. "The liking is mutual. I think myself fortunate in having you for my com panion."

"The luck is on my side, Mr. Spencer. What would I be but for you. I wouldn't be a tramp any more, for I am tired enough of that, but I should have to earn my living as a newsboy or a bootblack, and have no chance of getting an education."

So the relations between Tony and his new friend became daily more close, until Mr. Spencer came to regard him as a young brother, in whose progress he was warmly interested.

A tutor was selected, and Tony began to study. His ambition was roused. He realized for the first time how ignorant he was, and it is not too much to say that he learned in one month as much as most boys learn in three. He got rid of the uncouth words he had acquired in early life, and adapted his manners to the new position which he found him‧ self occupying in society. Mr. Spencer, too, was benefited by his new friend. He gave up drink and dissipation, and contented himself with pleasures in which he could invite Tony to participate.

Meanwhile Mr. Harvey Middleton and Rudolph had arrived in England, and we must leave our hero for a time and join them.

CHAPTER XXXII.

HOME AGAIN.

WHEN Mrs. Harvey Middleton reached England, she delayed but a day in London to attend to necessary business. This business was solely connected with her mission to America. Rudolph Rugg accompanied her to the chambers of a well-known lawyer, and testified to having had the charge of Tony, closing with the description of his death. Of course nothing was said of the well, or about his having thrown him in, for Rudolph was not a fool. The details of a probable story had been got up by Mrs. Middleton and Rugg in concert. According to them and the written testimony, Tony had been run over by a train on the Erie railway, and a newspaper paragraph describing such an accident to an un·known boy was produced in corroboration.

It was an ingenious fabrication, and Mrs. Middleton plumed herself upon it.

"Poor boy!" she said, with a hypocritical sigh, "his was a sad fate."

"It was, indeed," said the lawyer; "but," he added, dryly, "you have no cause to regret it, since it secures the estate."

"Don't mention it, Mr. Brief. It is sad to profit by such a tragedy."

"You don't take a business view of it, madame. Such things happen, and if we can't prevent them, we may as well profit by them."

"Of course I will not refuse what has fallen in my way," said Mrs. Middleton; "but I had formed the plan, if I found the boy alive, of bringing him home and educating him for his position. He would not have let me want."

"Don't she do it well, though?" thought Rudolph, who heard all this with a cynical admiration for the ex-governess. "If I was a gentleman, I'd make up to her, and make her Mrs. Rugg if she'd say the word."

"You think this man's evidence will substantiate my claim to the estate?" she asked, after a pause.

"I should say there was no doubt on that point, unless, of course, his evidence is impeached or contradicted."

"That is hardly likely, Mr. Brief. The poor man suffered much at the death of the boy, to whom he was ardently attached."

"So you loved the boy, Mr. Rugg?" said the lawyer.

"Oh, uncommon," said Rudolph. "He was my pet, and the apple of my eye. We was always together, Tony and I."

"And I suppose he loved you."

"He couldn't bear me out of his sight; he looked upon me as a father, sir."

"If he'd come into the estate, he would probably

have provided for you," suggested the lawyer, watching him keenly.

"It's likely, sir. I wish he had."

"So it's a personal loss to you—the death of the boy."

"Yes, sir."

"Mrs. Middleton probably will not forget your services to the boy."

"No, sir. I shall, of course, do something for Mr. Rugg, though not as much, perhaps, as my poor cousin would have done. Mr. Rugg, will you see me to my carriage?"

"Certainly, ma'am."

Mrs. Middleton was anxious to go away. The conversation had taken a turn which she did not like. It almost seemed as if the lawyer was trying to find out something, and she thought it best to get Rudolph away from the influence, lest Mr. Brief should catechise him, and draw out something to her disadvantage.

"Mr. Rugg," she said, as they were going down stairs, "I advise you not to go near Mr. Brief again."

"Why not, ma'am?"

"These lawyers are crafty. Before you knew what he was after, he would extract the secret from you, and there would be trouble for both of us."

"Do you think so, ma'am? I didn't see nothing of it?"

"I think he suspects something. That matters nothing if it does not go beyond suspicion. Unless he can impeach your testimony and draw you into contradictions. we are safe, and you are sure of an income for life."

"You needn't be afraid for me, ma'am. We are in the same boat."

She frowned a little at the familiar tone in which he spoke. It was as if he put himself on an equality with her. But it was true, nevertheless, and it was unpleasant for her to think of.

Was there nothing else that was unpleasant? Did she not think of the poor boy who, as she thought, was killed, and at her instigation? Yes, she thought often of him, but as much as she could she kept the subject away from her thoughts.

"He's better off," she said to herself. "He didn't know anything of the property, and he wasn't fit to possess it. All the troubles of life are over for him."

"What are your plans, Mr. Rugg?" she asked.

"I have a mind to go down to Middleton Hall with you, ma'am. I used to live there years ago, and I might find some of my old cronies."

"For that very reason you must not go," she said, hastily. "They would be asking you all sorts of questions. and you'd be letting out something."

"They wouldn't get nothing out of me."

"If you made no answer it would be as bad. They would suspect you."

"And you, too."

"Precisely."

" It's rather hard, Mrs. Middleton, I can't see my old friends."

" You can make new ones. A man with money can always find friends."

"That's true, ma'am," said Rudolph, brightening up. "Then you'd recommend me to stay in London?"

"In London, or anywhere else that you like better. Only don't come within twenty miles of Middleton Hall.

" Well, ma'am, you're wiser than I am, and you know better what it's best to do."

"Of course I do. You are safe in being guided by me."

" But about the money, ma'am. How am I to get that if I don't see you?"

"Once a quarter I will pay in forty pounds to your account at any bank you choose. You can let me know."

" All right, ma'am. It's strange to me to think of having a bank account."

"It need not be strange henceforth. And now, Mr. Rugg, we must part. I must hasten down to Middleton Hall to look after the estate. I have been absent from it now for nearly three months."

"I suppose you are in a hurry to see your young man," said Rudolph, with a grin.

" Mr. Rugg," said the lady, haughtily, "I beg you will make no reference to my private affairs. You speak as if I were a nursery maid.'

"I beg your pardon, ma'am. No offense was meant."

"Then none is taken. But remember my caution."

"She stepped into the hansom which was waiting for her, and Rudolph remained standing on the sidewalk."

"She's puttin' on airs," said the tramp, frowning. "She forgets all about her bein' a governess once, without five pounds in the world. She acts as if she were a lady born. I don't like it. She may try her airs on others, but not on Rudolph Rugg. He knows a little too much about Mrs. Harvey Middleton. Rich as you are, you're in his power, and if he was so inclined he could bring you down from your high place, so he could."

But Rudolph's anger was only transient. He was too astute not to understand clearly that he could not harm Mrs. Middleton without harming himself quite as much. As things stood, he was securely provided for. No more tramping about the country for him in all weathers. He had enough to lodge and feed him, and provide all the beer and tobacco he could use. This was certainly a comfortable reflection. So he sought out a comfortable lodging and installed himself before night, determined to get what enjoyment he could out of London and the income he had so foully won.

And Mrs. Middleton, she, too, congratulated herself.

She leaned back in the cab and gave herself up to

joyful anticipations of future happiness and security.

"Thank Heaven, I have got rid of that low fellow," she ejaculated, inwardly. I never want to see the brute again. He was necessary to my purpose, and I employed him, but I should be glad if he would get drowned, or be run over, or end his miserable life in some way, so that I might never see or hear of him again."

But the thought of Rudolph did not long trouble her. She thought rather of the handsome Captain Lovell, whom she loved, and to marry whom she had committed this crime, and the hard woman's face softened, and a smile crept over it.

"I shall soon see him, my Gregory," she murmured. "He will soon be mine, and I shall be repaid for my long, wearisome journey."

CHAPTER XXXIII.

CAPTAIN GREGORY LOVELL.

A CARRIAGE drove rapidly up the avenue leading to Middleton Hall.

The hall was not large, but was handsome and well proportioned, and looked singularly attractive, its gray walls forming a harmonious contrast with the bright green ivy that partially covered them, and the broad, smooth lawn that stretched out in front.

Mrs. Middleton regarded her home with unmingled satisfaction. It was to be her home now as long as she lived. Now that the boy was dead no one could wrest it from her. She would live there, but not in solitary grandeur. The news of her success would bring Captain Gregory Lovell to her side, and their marriage would follow as soon as decency would permit. If afterward he should desire to have the name of the residence changed to Lovell Hall, Mrs. Middleton decided that she would not object. Why should she? She had no superstitious love for her present name, while Lovell had for her the charm which love always gives to the name of the loved one.

The housekeeper, stout and matronly, received her mistress at the door.

"Welcome home, Mrs. Middleton," she said; "how long it seems since you went away."

"How do you do, Sarah," said her mistress, graciously. "I can assure you I am glad to be back."

"You will find everything in order, mum, I hope and believe," said Sarah. "We expected to see you sooner."

"I hoped to be back sooner, but the business detained me longer than I desired."

"And did you succeed, mum, if I may be so bold,' inquired the housekeeper, curiously.

"As I expected, Sarah. I found that the poor boy was dead."

"Indeed, mum."

"I hoped to bring him back with me, according to my poor husband's desire, but it was ordered otherwise by an inscrutable Providence."

Sarah coughed.

"It is very sad," she said, but she looked curiously at her mistress.

She knew very well that this sad news rejoiced the heart of Mrs. Middleton, and the latter knew that she could not for a moment impose upon her clear-sighted housekeeper. But the farce must be kept up for the sake of appearances.

"Come up to my chamber with me, Sarah. I want to ask you what has been going on since I went away? Have you heard from Lady Lovell's family? Are they all well?"

Lady Lovell was the mother of Captain Gregory Lovell, and the question was earnestly put.

"They are all well except the captain," answered Sarah.

"Is he sick?" demanded her mistress, turning upon her swiftly.

"No, mum; I only meant to say that the captain was gone away."

"Gone away! When? Where?"

"He's ordered to India, I believe, mum. He went away a month ago."

Mrs. Middleton sank into her chair, quite overcome. Her joy was clouded, for the reward of her long and toilsome journey was snatched from her.

"Did he not leave any message?" she asked. "Did he not call before he went away?"

"Yes, mum. He left a note."

"Give it to me quick. Why did you not mention it to me before?"

"It's the first chance I got, mum. The letter is in my own chamber. I took the best care of it. I will get it directly."

"Do go, Sarah."

Mrs. Middleton awaited the return of Sarah with nervous impatience. Perhaps the captain had thrown her over, after all, and, loving him as she did, this would have torn the heart of the intriguing woman, who, cold and selfish as she was so far as others were concerned, really loved the handsome captain.

Sarah speedily reappeared with the letter.

"Here it is, mum," she said. "I have taken the best care of it."

Mrs. Middleton tore it open with nervous haste This is the way it ran:

"MY DEAR JANE—I am about to set out for India —not willingly, but my regiment is ordered there, and I must obey or quit the service. This, as you well know, I cannot do; for apart from my official pay, I have but a paltry two hundred pounds a year, and that is barely enough to pay my tailor's bill. I am sorry to go away in your absence. If I were only sure you would bring home good news, I could afford to sell my commission and wait. But it is so uncertain that I cannot take the risk.

"I need not say, my dear Jane, how anxious I am to have all the impediments to our union removed. I am compelled to be mercenary. It is, alas! necessary for me, as a younger son, to marry a woman with money. I shall be happy, indeed, if interest and love go hand in hand, as they will if your absolute claim to your late husband's estate is proved beyond a doubt. I append my India address, and shall anxiously expect a communication from you on your return. If you have been successful, I will arrange to return at once, and our union can be solemnized without delay. Once more, farewell.

"Your devoted
"GREGORY LOVELL."

Mrs. Middleton, after reading this letter, breathed a sigh of relief. He was still hers, and she had only to call him back. There would be a vexatious delay, but that must be submitted to. She had feared to lose him, and this apprehension, at least, might be laid aside.

To some the letter would have seemed too mercenary. Even Mrs. Middleton could not help suspecting that, between love and interest, the latter was far the most powerful in the mind of Captain Lovell. But she purposely closed her eyes to this unpleasant suspicion. She was in love with the handsome captain, and it was the great object of her life to become his wife. She decided to answer the letter immediately.

Her desk was at hand, and she opened it at once, and wrote a brief letter to her absent lover:

"DEAR GREGORY—I have just returned. I am deeply disappointed to find you absent, for, my darling, I have succeeded. I have legal proof—proof that cannot be disputed—that the boy, my husband's cousin, is dead. The poor boy was accidentally killed. I have the sworn affidavit of the man who took him to America, and who was his constant companion there.

"It is a sad fate for the poor boy. I sincerely deplore his tragical end—he was run over by a train of cars—yet (is it wicked?), my grief is mitigated by the thought that it removes all obstacle to our union. I do not for an instant charge you with interested motives. I am sure of your love, but I also comprehend the necessities of your position. You have been brought up as a gentleman, and you have the tastes of a gentleman. You cannot surrender your social position. It is necessary that, if you marry, you should have an adequate income to live upon. My darling Gregory, I am proud and happy in the thought that I can make you such. You know my estate. The rental is two thousand pounds, and that is enough to maintain our social rank. Come home, then, as soon as you receive this letter. I am awaiting you impatiently, and can hardly reconcile myself to the delay that must be. Make it as short as possible, and let me hear from you at once.

"Your own,

"JANE MIDDLETON."

There was unexpected delay in the reception of this letter. It was three months before it came into the hands of Captain Lovell. When at length it was received, he read it with a mixture of emotions.

"Decidedly," he said, removing the cigar from his mouth, "the old girl is fond of me. I wish I were fond of her, for I suppose I must marry her. It will be rather a bad pill to swallow, but it is well gilded. Two thousand pounds a year are not to be thrown away by a fellow in my straits. The prospect might be brighter, but I suppose I have no right to complain. It will make me comfortable for life. I must take care to have the estate settled upon me, and then the sooner the old girl dies the better."

So Captain Lovell wrote at once, saying that he would return home as soon as he could make ar-

rangements for doing so—that every day would
seem a month till he could once more embrace his
dear Jane.   The letter was signed, "Your devoted
Gregory."

Mrs. Middleton read it with unfeigned delight.
Her plans had succeeded, and the reward would
soon be hers.

But there was fresh delay.   Arrangements to return could not be made so easily as Captain Lovell
anticipated.   It was seven months from the day
Mrs. Middleton reached England when Captain
Lovell was driven to his hotel in London.   Meanwhile events had occurred which were to have an
effect upon Mrs. Middleton's plans.

CHAPTER XXXIV.

TONY ASTONISHES HIS OLD FRIENDS.

"Tony," said George Spencer one evening, "you have been making wonderful progress in your studies. In six months you have accomplished as much as I did at boarding school in two years when at your age."

"Do you really mean it, Mr. Spencer?" said Tony, gratified.

"I am quite in earnest."

"I am very glad of it," said Tony. "When I began I was almost discouraged. I was so much behind boys of my age."

"And now your attainements raise you above the average. Your tutor told me so yesterday when I made inquiries."

"I am rejoiced to hear it, Mr. Spencer, I was very much ashamed of myself at first, and I did not like to speak before your friends for fear they would find out what sort of a life I led. That is what made me work so hard."

"Well, Tony, you may congratulate yourself on having succeeded. I think you can venture now to take a little vacation."

"A vacation! I don't need one."

"Suppose it were spent in Europe?"

"What!" exclaimed Tony, eagerly, "you don't think of our going abroad?"

"Yes. The house with which I am connected wants me to go abroad on business. If I go you may go with me if you would like it."

"Like it!" exclaimed Tony, impetuously. "There is nothing I would like better."

"So I supposed," said George Spencer, smiling. "I may as well tell you that our passage is taken for next Saturday, by the Russia."

"And this is Monday evening. How soon it seems!"

"There won't be much preparation to make—merely packing your trunk."

"Mr. Spencer," said Tony, "I want to ask a favor."

"What is it?"

"I have told you about being employed at a country hotel, just before I came to the city and found you."

"Yes.

"I would like to go back there for a day, just to see how all my old friends are."

"You don't mean to apply again for your old place?"

"Not unless you turn me off, and I have to find work somewhere."

"Turn you off, Tony! Why, I shouldn't know how to get along without you. You are like a younger brother to me," said the young man, earnestly.

"Thank you, Mr. Spencer. You seem like an older brother to me. Sometimes I can hardly believe that I was once a tramp."

"It was your misfortune, Tony, not your fault. So you want to go back and view your former home?"

"Yes, Mr. Spencer."

"Then you had better start to-morrow morning, so as to be back in good time to prepare for the journey."

"Do you know, Mr. Spencer," said Tony, "Ive got an idea. I'll go back wearing the same clothes I had on when I left there."

"Have you got them still?"

"Yes, I laid them away, just to remind me of my old life. I'll take my other clothes in a bundle, and after a while I can put them on."

"What is your idea in doing this, Tony?" asked the young man.

"I want to give them a surprise."

"Very well, do as you please. Only don't stay away too long."

*   *   *   *   *   *

Tony proceeded to carry out the plan he had proposed.

He traveled by rail to a village near by, and then with his bundle suspended to a stick, took up his march to the tavern.

He entered the familiar stable yard. All looked as it did the day he left. There was only one person in the yard, and that one Tony recognized at once as his old enemy, Sam Payson, who appeared to be filling his old position, as stable boy.

"Hallo, Sam!" said Tony, whose entrance had not been observed.

Sam looked up and whistled.

"What, have you come back?" he said, not appearing overjoyed at the sight of Tony.

"Yes, Sam," said Tony.

"Where have you been all the time?"

"In New York part of the time."

"What have you been doing for a living?"

"Well, I lived with a gentleman there."

"What did you do—black his boots?"

"Not exactly."

"Did he turn you off?"

"No; but he's going to Europe next Saturday."

"So you're out of a place?"

"I have no employment."

"What made you come back here?" demanded Sam, suspiciously.

"I thought I'd like to see you all again."

"That don't go down," said Sam roughly. I know well enough what you're after."

"What am I after?"

"You're after my place. You're hoping Mr. Porter will take you on again. But it's no use. There ain't any chance for you."

"How long have you been back again, Sam?"

"Three months, and I am going to stay, too. You got me turned off once, but you can't do it again."

"I don't want to."

"Oh, no, I presume not," sneered Sam. "Of course, you don't. You've got on the same clothes you wore away, haven't you?"

"Yes, it's the same suit, but I've got some more things in my bundle."

"I guess you haven't made your fortune, **by the looks.**"

"The fact is, Sam, I haven't earned much since I went away."

"I knew you wouldn't. You ain't so smart as people think."

"I didn't know anybody thought me smart."

"James, the hostler, is always talking you up to me, but I guess I can rub along as well as you."

"You talk as if I was your enemy, Sam, instead of your friend."

"I don't want such a friend. You're after my place, in spite of all you say."

Just then James, the hostler, came out of the stable.

"What, is it you, Tony?" he asked, cordially.

"Yes, James; I hope you're well."

"Tip-top; and how are you?" asked the hostler, examining Tony, critically.

"I'm well."

"Have you been doing well?"

"I haven't wanted for anything. I've been with a gentleman in New York."

Here Mr. Porter appeared on the scene.

He too, recognized Tony.

"What! back again, Tony?" he said.

"I thought I'd just look in, sir."

" Do you want a place? "

" What sort of a place?"

" Your old place."

Sam heard this, and looked the picture of dismay. He took it for granted that Tony would accept at once, and privately determined that if he did he would give him a flogging, if it were a possible thing.

He was both relieved and surprised when Tony answered:

"I am much obliged to you, Mr. Porter, but I wouldn't like to cut out Sam. Besides, I have a place engaged in New York."

"I would rather have you than Sam, any day."

" Thank you, sir, but I've made an arrangement, and can't break it."

" How long are you going to stay here?"

" If you've a spare room, I'll stay over till to-morrow."

" All right. Go into the office, and they'll give you one."

" I say, Tony," said Sam, after the landlord had gone, "you're a better fellow than I thought you were. I thought you'd take my place when it was offered you."

" You see you were mistaken, Sam. I'll see you again."

Tony went into the hotel—went up to a small chamber that had been assigned him, changed his clothes for a handsome suit in his bundle, took a handsome gold watch and chain from his pocket and displayed them on his vest, and then came down again.

As he entered the yard again, Sam stared in amazement.

"It can't be you, Tony!" he said. "Where'd you get them clothes, and that watch?"

"I came by them honestly, Sam."

"But I can't understand it," said Sam, scratching his head. "Aint you poor, and out of work?"

"I'm out of work, but not poor. I've been adopted by a rich gentleman, and am going to sail for Europe on Saturday."

"Cracky! who ever heard the like? Wouldn't he adopt me, too?"

"I believe there is no vacancy," said Tony, smiling.

"Was that the reason you wouldn't take my place?"

"One reason."

"James!" called Sam, "just look at Tony now."

James stared, and when an explanation was made, heartily congratulated our hero.

"Sam," said Tony, producing a couple of showy neck-ties, "to prove to you that I am not your enemy, I have brought you these."

"They're stunning!" exclaimed the enraptured Sam. "I always thought you was a good fellow, Tony. Are they really for me?"

"To be sure they are, but I'm afraid, Sam, you didn't always think quite so well of me."

"Well, I do now.   You're a trump."

"And, James, I've brought you a present too."
Here Tony produced a handsome silver watch with
a silver chain appended.   "It's to remember me by."

"I'd remember you without it, Tony, but I'm very
much obliged too.   It's a real beauty."

When the landlord was told of Tony's good fortune, he was as much surprised as the rest.   Our
hero was at once changed to the handsomest room
in the hotel, and was made quite a lion during the
remainder of his stay.

There is something in success after all.

"Good-by, Tony," said Sam heartily, when our
hero left the next day.   You're a gentleman, and
I always said so."

"Thank you, Sam. Good luck to you!" responded
Tony, smiling.

"I'm a much finer fellow than when I was a
tramp," he said to himself.   "Sam says so, and he
ought to know. I suppose it's the way of the world.
And now for Europe!"

CHAPTER XXXV.

TONY'S BAD LUCK.

Two weeks later Tony and his friend were guests at a popular London hotel, not far from Charing Cross.

"We will postpone business till we have seen a little of London," said George Spencer. "Luckily my business is not of a pressing character, and it can wait."

"You have been in London before, Mr. Spencer," said Tony. "I am afraid you will find it a bore going round with me."

"Not at all. I spent a week here when a boy of twelve, and saw nothing thoroughly, so I am at your disposal. Where shall we go first?"

"I should like to see Buckingham Palace, where the queen lives."

"She doesn't live there much. However, we'll go to see it, but we'll take the Parliament House and Westminster Abbey on the way."

In accordance with this programme they walked —for the distance was but short—to Westminster Abbey. It would be out of place for me to describe here that wonderful church where so much of the rank and talent of past ages lies buried. It is enough to say that Tony enjoyed it highly. He afterward visited the Parliament House. This occupied another hour. When they came out Mr. Spencer said:

"Tony, I have got to go to my banker's. Do you care to come?"

"No, thank you, Mr. Spencer, I would rather walk round by myself."

"Very well, Tony, just as you please. Only don't get lost."

"I'll take care of that; I'm used to cities."

"You are not used to London. It is one of the blindest cities in the world; it is a complete labyrinth."

"I don't mean to get lost. You'll find me at the hotel at four o'clock."

"Very well. That will be early enough."

So George Spencer went his way, and Tony set out upon his rambles.

He found plenty to amuse him in the various buildings and sights of the great metropolis. But after awhile he began to wonder where he was. He had strayed into a narrow street, scarcely more than a lane, with a row of tumble-down dwellings on either side.

"There's nothing worth seeing here," said our hero. "I'll inquire my way to Charing Cross."

He went into a small beer house, and preferred his request."

"Charing Cross!" repeated the publican. It's a good ways from 'ere."

"How far?" asked Tony.

"A mile easy, and there's no end of turns."

"Just start me, then," said Tony, "and I'll reach there. Which way is it?"

"Turn to the left when you go out of this shop."

"All right, and thank you."

Tony noticed that there were three or four men seated at tables in the back part of the shop, but he had not the curiosity to look at them. If he had, he would have been startled, for among these men was Rudolph Rugg, more disreputable than ever in appearance, for he had been drinking deeply for the last six months. He stared at Tony as one dazed, for he supposed him dead long ago at the bottom of a well three thousand miles away.

"What's the matter, Rugg?" asked his companion. "You look as if you'd seen a ghost."

"So I have," muttered Rugg, starting for the door.

"Where are you going?"

"I've got a headache," said Rudolph.

"You've left your drink."

"I don't want it."

"What's come over him?" said his late companion, in surprise.

"No matter. He'll be back soon."

Rudolph swiftly followed Tony. He wanted to find out whether it was really the boy whom he had sought to murder or not. Then what did his appearance in London mean? Was he possibly in search of him—Rugg? It was wonderful, certainly. How had he obtained the means of coming to England? —as a gentleman, too, for Rudolph had not failed to notice his rich clothes. Had he obtained rich and powerful friends, and was he in search of the inheritance that had been wrongfully kept from him ?

Rudolph asked himself all these questions, but he could not answer one.

"If I could only ask him," he thought, "but that wouldn't be safe."

By this time he had come in sight of Tony, who was walking along slowly, not feeling in any particular hurry.

An idea struck Rudolph.

A boy who had been employed in begging was standing on the sidewalk.

"Gi'me a penny, sir," he said.

Rudolph paused.

"Walk along with me, and I'll show you how you can earn half a crown," he said.

"Will you ?" said the boy, his face brightening.

"Yes, I will, and you won't find it hard work, either."

"Go ahead, gov'nor."

"Do you see that boy ahead ?"

"That young gentleman ?"

"Yes," said Rudolph.

"I see him."

"I want you to manage to get him up to my room; it's No. 7 —— street, top floor, just at the head of the stairs."

"Shall I tell him you want to see him ?"

"No, he wouldn't come. Tell him your poor

grandfather is sick in bed—anything you like, only get him to come."

"S'posin' he won't come?"

"Then follow him, and find out where he is staying. Do you understand?"

"Yes, gov'nor. I'll bring him."

"Go ahead, and I'll hurry round to the room. I'll be in bed."

"All right."

The boy was a sharp specimen of the juvenile London beggar. He was up to the usual tricks of his class, and quite competent to the task which Rudolph had engaged him to perform."

He came up to Tony, and then began to whimper.

"What's the matter, Johnny?" said Tony, addressing him by the usual New York name for an unknown boy.

"Oh, my poor grandfather is so sick," said the boy.

"What's the matter with him?"

"I don't know. I guess he's goin' to die."

"Why don't you send for a doctor?"

"He would't come—we're so poor."

"Do you live near here?"

"Oh, yes, sir; only a little way."

"I want to go to Charing Cross—is it much out of the way?"

"No, sir; it's right on the way there."

"Then, if you'll show me the way to Charing Cross afterward. I will go round with you and look at your grandfather. Perhaps I can do something for him."

"Oh, sir, how kind you are! I know'd you was a gentleman when I fust saw you."

" When was your grandfather taken sick ?"

"Two days ago," said the boy.

"Is he in bed ?"

"Yes, sir. Leastways, he was when I came out. We didn't have no breakfast."

"I am sorry for that. Don't you want to buy something to take to him ?"

"If you'll give me a shillin', sir, I'll ask him what he can eat. Sick folks can't eat the same things as the rest of us."

"To be sure. You are right. Well, here's a shilling."

"The boy little thinks that I have known many a time what it is to be without breakfast or money to buy any," thought Tony. "I'll do something for the poor man, if only to show how grateful I am for my own good fortune."

He followed the boy for about ten minutes, until they reached rather a shabby building. This was No. 7.

"Come right up after me," said the boy.

The two went up till they reached the room indicated by Rudolph. The boy pushed the door open.

A sound of groaning proceeded from the bed.

"Grandfather, I've brought a kind young gentleman," said the boy.

"Come here," muttered the person in bed.

Tony came up to the bed.

In an instant Rudolph had thrown off the clothes and had him seized by the arm.

"There's your money, boy. Go!" he said to the other, flinging a half-crown."

"I've got you at last!" he shouted. "Now, you young villain, I'll get even with you!"

His face was almost fiendish with rage, as he uttered these words.

CHAPTER XXXVI.

"I HATE YOU!"

To say that Tony was not startled would not be true. Without a moment's warning he found himself in the power of his old enemy—completely in his power, knowing, too, the desperate character of the man, which would let him stick at nothing.

Rudolph enjoyed his evident surprise.

"I've been waiting for this," he said. "It's a great joy to me to have you here in my power."

By this time Tony had collected himself, and had become composed.

"Rudolph," he said, "what makes you hate me so?"

"Haven't you tried to injure me—didn't you get me arrested? Do you forget that night in the old miser's hut?"

"No, I don't forget it, but you forced me to act as I did. But even if I did injure you, you took your revenge."

"When, and how?"

"When you threw me into the well. How could you do such a dark deed? What had I done that you should seek to murder me?"

"How did you get out?" asked Rudolph, giving way to curiosity.

"I climbed out."

"How?"

"By means of the wall that lined the well. Finally I got hold of the rope."

"So that was the way, was it? I ought to have made surer of your fate."

"How could you do that?"

"By throwing some rocks down on you," answered the tramp, with a malignant frown.

"I am glad I have not such a wicked disposition as you, Rudolph," said Tony, looking at him fix edly.

"Take care how you insult me, boy!" said Rudolph, angrily.

"I have no wish to insult you. Now tell me why you have lured me here? I suppose you hired the boy."

"I did, and he did the work well," said the tramp, triumphantly.

"Well, now I am here, what do you want of me?"

"First, tell me how you happen to be in London? Did you know I was here?"

"I knew you crossed the Atlantic."

"How?"

"I saw you buy your ticket."

"What?" exclaimed the tramp, in surprise. "Did you reach New York so soon?"

"Yes. I lost my situation at the inn, for they did not believe my story about having been thrown down the well by a Quaker."

Rudolph laughed.

" It was a good disguise," he said.   " So they discharged you?   That was good."

" I did not think so at the time, but it proved to be the luckiest thing that could happen to me."

" How was that?"

" It led me to go to New York.   There I found a rich and generous friend.   I have been with him ever since."

" As a servant?"

" No; as his adopted brother.   He supplied me with teachers, and in little more than six months I have acquired as much as most boys do in two or three years."

" So you have gone in for education, have you?" said Rudolph, sneering.

" Yes.   Could I go in for anything better?"

" And you consider yourself a young gentleman, now, do you?"

" That is the rank I hold in society," said Tony, calmly.

" And you forget that you were once Tony, the Tramp?"

" No, Rudolph, I have not forgotten that.   It was not my fault, and I am not ashamed of it.   But I should be ashamed if I had not left that kind of life as soon as I was able."

" By Heaven, you shall go back to it! " said Rudolph, malignantly.

" I never will," answered Tony, gently, but firmly.

"I will force you to it."

"Neither you nor any one else can force me to it. I will black boots in the street first."

"That will suit me just as well," said the tramp, laughing maliciously. You have grown too proud. I want to lower your pride, young popinjay."

"I am not afraid of anything you can do to me, Rudolph," said Tony, bravely.

"Suppose I choose to kill you?"

"You won't dare do it. We are not in the woods now."

Tony had hit the truth. Rudolph did not dare to kill him, though he would have been glad to. But he knew that he would himself be arrested, and he had more to live for now than formerly. He had an income, and comfortably provided for, and he did not choose to give up this comfortable and independent life.

"No," he said, "I won't kill you; but I will be revenged for all that. First, I will keep you from that generous friend of yours."

"What will he think has become of me?" thought Tony, uneasily.

A thought came to him. He would appeal to the man's love of money.

"Rudolph," he said, "I am afraid my friend will be uneasy about me. If you will let me go I will give you ten pounds that I have in my pocket."

"I don't believe you have so much money," said Rudolph, cunningly.

Tony fell into the snare unsuspectingly. He

drew out his pocket-book and displayed two five-pound notes on the Bank of England.

Rudolph quickly snatched them from him.

"They are mine already," he said, with a mocking laugh.

"So I see," said Tony, coolly; "but I was about to offer you fifty pounds besides."

"Have you the money in your pocketbook?"

"No, I haven't, but I could get it from Mr. Spencer."

"It don't go down, Tony," said Rudolph, shaking his head. "I am not so much in need of money as to pay so dearly for it. Listen to me. If you have been lucky, so have I. I have an income, safe and sure, of one hundred and fifty pounds."

"You have!" exclaimed Tony, surprised.

"Yes."

"Do you hold any position?"

"No; I merely promise to keep my mouth shut."

"Is it about me?"

"Yes. The long and short of it is that there is an English estate, bringing in two thousand pounds rental, that of right belongs to you."

"To me—an estate of two thousand pounds a year?" exclaimed Tony, in astonishment.

"Yes; the party who owns it pays me an income as hush money. I have only to say the word, and the estate will be yours, Tony."

"Say the word, Rudolph, and you shall have the same income," entreated Tony. "It isn't the money I so much care for, but I want to know who I am.

I want to be restored to my rightful place in society. Is my mother living?"

"No."

"Nor my father?"

'No."

Tony looked sober.

"Then I should not care so much for the money.
Still it ought to be mine.

"Of course it ought," said Rudolph, gloating over
the boy's emotion.

"You shall lose nothing by telling me—by be-
coming my friend. I will never refer to the past—
never speak of what happened in America."

"No doubt," sneered Rudolph, "but it can't be."

"Why can't it be?"

"*Because I hate you!*" hissed the tramp, with a
baleful look. "Not another word. It's no use, I
shall lock you up here for the present, while I am
out. When I come back I will let you know what
I am going to do to you."

He left the room, locking the door behind him.

Tony sat down to reflect upon the strange position in which he was placed.

CHAPTER XXXVII.

MRS. MIDDLETON AND HER LOVER.

WHEN Rudolph left Tony imprisoned, he began to think over the situation with regard to his own interest.

He was already dissatisfied with the income he received from Mrs. Middleton; though at the time it seemed to him large, he found that he could easily spend more. He did not have expensive lodgings—in fact, they were plain, and quite within his means, but he drank and gambled, and both these amusements were expensive. He had already made up his mind to ask for a larger income, and Tony's offer stimulated him to ask at once.

"If Mrs. Middleton won't, the boy will," he said to himself.

Mrs. Middleton was in London, In fact, at that moment she was conversing with Captain Lovell, to whom she had been formally betrothed. He had satisfied himself that the prospects were all right, and then had renewed his offer. The marriage was to take place in a month, and Mrs. Middleton was in town to make suitable preparations for it. She was perfectly happy, for she was about to marry a man she loved.

As for Captain Lovell, he was well enough contented. He did not care much for the lady as regards love, but he was decidedly in love with her property.

"It will make me comfortable for life," he said, with a shrug of the shoulders, "and after marriage I can pay as little attention to Mrs. Lovell as I choose. She must be content with marrying my name."

The widow had taken handsome apartments at a West End boarding house. There she received callers.

Captain Lovell was lounging in an easy chair, looking rather bored. His *fiancee* was inspecting an array of dry goods which had been sent in from a fancy London shop.

"Don't you think this silk elegant, Gregory!" she asked, displaying a pattern.

" Oh, ah, yes, I suppose so,"'he answered with a yawn.

"I would like to have your taste, Gregory."

"I have no taste, my dear Mrs. Middleton, about such matters."

" Don't you think it will become me?"

" Why, to be sure; everything becomes you, **you** know."

She laughed.

" Would a yellow turban become me?" she asked.

" Well, perhaps not," he said, "but of course you know best."

" How little you men know about a lady's dress!"

"I should think so. The fact is, my dear Mrs. Middleton, that part of my education was neglected."

"When I am your wife, Gregory, I shall always appeal to your taste."

"Will you?" he said, rather frightened. 'Pon my honor, I hope you won't now."

"And I shall expect you to consult me about your wardrobe."

"What, about my trousers and coats? Really, that's very amusing; 'pon my honor it is."

"Don't you think I feel an interest in how my dear Gregory is dressed?"

"I don't know, I'm sure."

"But I do, and shall I tell you why?"

"If you want to."

"Because I love you," she said softly, and she rose from her chair, and crossing, laid her hand affectionately on his shoulder.

He shrank, just the least in the world, and felt annoyed, but didn't like to say so. She might be angry, and though he did not love her, he did want to marry her, and so escape from his money troubles."

"Of course, I'm ever so much obliged to you," he said, "and all that sort of thing."

"And you love me, Gregory, don't you?" she asked, tenderly.

"Did You ever ! I wish she'd stop," he said to himself. "She makes me awful uncomfortable."

"Don't you love me, Gregory?"

"If I didn't love you, do you think I would have

asked you to become Mrs. Lovell?" he said, evading the question.

"To be sure, Gregory," she replied, trying to look satisfied.

"And now I must go; I must, 'pon my honor," he said, rising.

"You have been here so short a time," she pleaded.

"But I promised to be at the club. I'm to meet a fellow officer, and it's the hour now.

"Then I must let you go. But you'll come again soon?"

"Yes, 'pon honor," and the captain kissed his hand to his *fiancee*.

"I wonder if he really loves me!" she said to herself, wistfully.

At this moment the servant entered.

"Please, ma'am, there's a rough-looking man below, who says he wants to see you. His name is Rugg."

"Admit him," said Mrs. Middleton, looking annoyed.

CHAPTER XXXVIII.

A STORMY INTERVIEW.

"Why are you here Mr. Rugg?" demanded Mrs. Middleton, coolly.

"On business," said the tramp, throwing himself, uninvited upon the same chair from which Captain Lovell had just risen.

Mrs. Middleton flushed with anger, but she did not dare to treat his insolence as it deserved.

"What business can you have with me?" she asked, coldly.

"It's about the allowance."

"It was paid punctually, was it not?"

"Yes."

"Then you can have no business with me. Have I not told you that you are not to call upon me at any time? My agent attends to that."

"I want the allowance raised," said Rudolph, abruptly.

"Raised?"

"Yes, you must double it."

Mrs. Middleton was now really angry.

"I never heard such insolence," she said. "You have taken your trouble for nothing. I shall not give you a pound more."

"You'd better, Mrs. Middleton," said Rudolph, "or I may tell all I know."

"You would only ruin yourself, and lose your entire income."

"I should ruin you, too."

"Not at all. No one would believe you against me. Besides, are you ready to be tried for murder?"

"Who has committed murder?"

"You have."

"Prove it."

"Didn't you kill the boy?"

"No."

"You swore to me he was dead."

"Suppose he didn't die."

"You are wasting your time, Mr. Rugg," said Mrs. Middleton, coldly. "Of course I understand your motives. You have been extravagant, and wasted your money, hoping to get more out of me. But it is useless."

"You'll be sorry for this, ma'am," said Rugg, angrily.

"I don't think I shall. Before doing anything that *you* will be sorry for, consider that to a man in your position the income I give you is very liberal."

"Liberal! It isn't one-tenth of what you get."

"Very true, but the case is different."

"You may believe me or not, but the boy is alive, and I know where he is."

Mrs. Middleton did not believe one word of what he said. She was convinced that Tony had been killed by the man before her, and was indignant at the trick which she thought he was trying to play upon her. She felt that if she yielded to his importunity, it would only be the beginning of a series of demands. She had courage and firmness, and she decided to discourage him once for all in his exactions.

"I don't believe you," she said, "and I am not afraid."

"Then you won't increase my income," he said.

"No, I will not. Neither now nor at any other time will I do it. What I have agreed to do I will do, but I will not give you a penny more. Do you understand me, Mr Rugg?"

"I believe I do," said Rudolph, rising, "and I tell you you'll be sorry for what you are saying."

"I will take the risk," she said, contemptuously.

Rudolph's face was distorted with passion as he left the room.

"I hate her more than the boy," he muttered. "He shall have the estate."

CHAPTER XXXIX.

TONY'S ESCAPE.

WHEN Tony found himself left a prisoner in his enemy's room, he did not immediately make an effort to escape. In fact, he did not feel particularly alarmed.

"I am in a large city, and there are other lodgers in this building. There can be no danger. I will wait awhile and think over what Rudolph has told me. Can it be true that I am heir to a large estate in England, and that he can restore me to it if he will? He can have no motive for deceiving me. It must be true."

Tony felt that he would give a great deal to know more. Where was this estate, and who now held it? It occurred to him that somewhere about the room he might find some clew to the mystery. He immediately began to explore it.

Rudolph was not a literary man. He had neither books nor papers whose tell-tale testimony might convict him. In fact, the best of his personal possessions was very small. A few clothes were lying about the room. Tony decided to examine the pockets of these, in the hope of discovering something in his interest. Finally, he found in the pocket of a shooting coat a small memorandum book, in which a few entries, chiefly of bets, had been made. In these Tony felt no interest, and he was about to throw down the book, when his eye caught this entry:

"Dead broke. Must write to Mrs. Middleton for more money."

Tony's heart beat rapidly.

This must be the person from whom Rudolph received his income, and, by consequence the person who was in fraudulent possession of the estate that was rightfully his.

"Mrs. Middleton!"

"I wish I knew where she lives," thought our hero. "No doubt there are hundreds of the name in England."

This might be, but probably there was but one Mrs. Middleton in the possession of an estate worth two thousand pounds rental.

"I am on the track," thought Tony. "Now let me get away, and consult George Spencer."

It was easier said than done. The door was locked, and it was too strong to break down.

"There must be somebody in the room below," thought Tony. "I'll pound till they hear me."

He jumped up and down with such force that it did attract attention in the room below. Presently he heard a querulous voice at the key-hole:

"What's the matter? Are you mad?"

"No, but I'm locked in," said Tony. "Can't you let me out?"

"I have no key to the door, but the landlady has."

"Won't you please to ask her to let me out? I'll be ever so much obliged."

"Stop pounding then."

"I will."

Scarcely two minutes had elapsed when a key was heard in the lock and the door was opened.

"How came you here, sir?" asked the landlady, a short, stout woman—suspiciously.

"The gentleman locked me in—in a joke," said Tony.

"Maybe you're a burglar," said the landlady, eyeing him doubtfully.

Tony laughed.

"Do I look like it?" he asked.

"Well, no," the landlady admitted, "but appearances are deceitful."

"Not with me, I assure you. I am really sorry to put you to so much trouble to let me out. Won't you accept of this?" and Tony produced a half sovereign.

"Really, sir, I see that you are quite the gentleman," said the landlady, pocketing the piece with avidity. "Can't I do anything for you?"

"Only, if you'll be kind enough to give this to the gentleman when he returns."

Tony hastily wrote a line on a card, and gave it to the now complacent dame.

Fifteen minutes after Tony's departure Rudolph returned.

He sprang up stairs only to find the room empty and the bird flown.

"What's come of the boy!" he exclaimed in dismay; "how did he get out?"

He summoned the landlady quickly.

"Do you know anything of the boy that was in my room, Mrs. Jones?"

"Yes, Mr. Rugg, I let him out. He said you locked him in in fun.

"Humph! what else did he say?"

"He left this card for you."

Rugg seized it hastily, and read with startled eyes:

"I am at Morley's. Come and see me soon, or I will go to Mrs. Middleton.

"TONY."

"Confusion! where did the boy find out?" thought the tramp. "I must do something, or I am ruined."

It was a mystery to him how Tony had learned so much, and he naturally concluded that he knew a good deal more. He felt that no time was to be lost, and started at once for Morley's. Inquiring for Tony, he was at once admitted to the presence of Tony and George Spencer.

"So you got my card!" said Tony.

"Yes. What do you know about Mrs. Middleton?" demanded Rudolph.

"That she possesses the estate that ought to be mine. That's about it, isn't it?"

"Yes," said Rudolph, "but you can't get it without me?"

"Why not?"

"I was the man that was hired to abduct you when you was a boy."

"Can you prove that?" asked Spencer.

"I can."

"Will your story be believed?"

"Yes. The tenantry will remember me. I was one of them at the time."

"Are you ready to help my young friend here to recover his rights?" asked Spencer.

"This morning I said no. Now I say yes, if he'll do the fair thing by me."

A conference was entered into and a bargain was finally made. Rudolph was to receive two hundred pounds a year as a reward for his services, if successful.

When this arrangement had been completed, an appointment was made for the next morning; at which hour a lawyer of repute was also present. After listening attentively to Rudolph's statement, he said, decisively:

"Your young friend has a strong case, but I advise you to see Mrs. Middleton privately. It may not be necessary to bring the matter into court; and this would be preferable, as it would avoid scandal."

"I put myself in your hands," said Tony, promptly.

"Mrs. Harvey Middleton is in London," said the lawyer. "I will call this afternoon."

CHAPTER XL.

ALL'S WELL THAT ENDS WELL.

Mrs. Harvey Middleton sat in her boudoir, trying to read a novel. But it failed to interest her. She felt uneasy, she scarcely knew why. The evening previous she had been at the Haymarket Theatre, and had been struck by a boy's face. Ten feet from her sat Tony, with his friend, George Spencer. He looked wonderfully like his father, as she remembered him, and she was startled. She did not know Tony, but Rugg's angry warning struck her.

"Was he right? Can this be the boy I have so much reason to dread?" she asked herself.

She was thinking of this when the servant entered the room with a card.

"C. Barry," she repeated, "wishes to see Mrs. Middleton on business of the greatest importance."

"Ask him to come up," she said, uneasily.

It was the lawyer, as the reader may have suspected.

"Mrs. Middleton," he said, with a bow, "I must apologize for my intrusion."

"You say your business is important," said the lady.

"It is—of the first importance."

"Explain yourself, I beg."

"I appear before you, madame, in behalf of your late husband's cousin, Anthony Middleton, who is the heir of the estate which you hold in trust."

It was out now, and Mrs. Middleton was at bay.

"There is no such person," she said. "The boy you refer to is dead."

"What proof have you of his decease?"

"I have the sworn statement of the man who saw him die."

"And this man's name?"

"Is Rudolph Rugg."

"I thought so. Mr. Rugg swore falsely. He is ready to contradict his former statement."

"He has been tampered with!" exclaimed Mrs. Middleton, pale with passion.

"That may be," said the lawyer; but he added, significantly, "Not by us."

"The boy is an impostor," said Mrs. Middleton, hotly. "I will not surrender the estate."

"I feel for your disappointment, madame; but I think you are hasty."

"Who will believe the statement of a common tramp?"

"You relied upon it before, madame. But we have other evidence," continued the lawyer.

"What other evidence?"

"The striking resemblance of my young friend to the family."

"Was—was he at the Haymarket Theatre last evening?"

"He was. Did you see him?"

"I saw the boy I suppose you mean. He had a slight look like Mr. Middleton."

"He is his image."

"Suppose—suppose this story to be true, what do you offer me?" asked Mrs. Middleton, sullenly.

"An income of three hundred pounds from the estate," said the lawyer. "If the matter comes to court, this Rugg, I am bound to tell you, has an ugly story to tell, in which you are implicated."

Mrs. Middleton knew well enough what it meant. If the conspiracy should be disclosed, she would be ostracised socially. She rapidly made up her mind.

"Mr. Barry," she said, "I will accept your terms, on a single condition."

"Name it, madame."

"That you will give me six weeks' undisturbed possession of the estate, keeping this matter secret meanwhile."

"If I knew your motive, I might consent."

"I will tell you in confidence. Within that time I am to be married. The abrupt disclosure of this matter might break off the marriage."

"May I ask the name of the bridegroom?"

"Captain Gregory Lovell."

The lawyer smiled. He knew of Captain Lovell, and owed him a grudge. He suspected that the captain was mercenary in his wooing, and he thought that it would be a fitting revenge to let matters go on."

"I consent, upon my own responsibility," he said.

"Thank you," said Mrs. Middleton, with real gratitude.

She would not lose the man she loved, after all.

* * * * * * *

A month later the marriage of Captain Gregory Lovell, of Her Majesty's service, and Mrs. Harvey Middleton, of Middleton Hall, was celebrated. There was a long paragraph in the Morning "Post," and Mrs. Lovell was happy.

When, a week later, at Paris, the gallant captain was informed of the trick that had been played upon him, there was a terrible scene. He cursed his wife, and threatened to leave her.

"But, Gregory, I have three hundred pounds income," she pleaded. "We can live abroad."

"And I have sold myself for that paltry sum!" he said, bitterly.

But he concluded to make the best of a bad bargain. Between them they had an income of five hundred pounds, and on this they made shift abroad, where living is cheap. But the marriage was not happy. He was brutal at times, and his wife realized sadly that he had never loved her. But she has all the happiness she deserves, and so has he.

Rudolph drank himself to death in six months. So the income which he was to receive made but a slight draft upon the Middleton estate.

And Tony!—no longer Tony the Tramp, but the Hon. Anthony Middleton, of Middleton Hall—he has just completed a course at Oxford, and is now the possessor of an education which will help fit him for the responsibilities he is to assume. His frank, off-hand manner makes him an immense favorite with the circle to which he now belongs. He says little of his early history, and it is seldom thought of now. He has made a promise to his good friend, George Spencer, to visit the United States, and will doubtless do so. He means at that time to visit once more the scenes with which he became familiar when he was A Poor Boy.

WHITMARSH'S REVENGE.

Roger Blake and Belcher Whitmarsh were both
called quite good boys, but for different reasons.
As their friends used sometimes to put it, Belcher
was liked *because* of his temper, and Roger was liked
in spite of his temper.

Roger was quick to fly into a passion, and as
quick to get over it, while Belcher was almost
always good natured, but when once really offended
remembered the offense like an Indian.

The broad play-green in front of the country
schoolhouse, where the boys spent their term times
together, was surrounded by trees and rocky pasture lots. A pretty brook ran through it. On the
sides of the brook and in the rain-gulleys there were
plenty of pebbles and small stones.

One noon, when the boys had begun a trial of
skill in firing stones at a mark, an unlucky turn was
given to this small "artillery practice" by the
thoughtless challenge of one of the youngsters to a
playmate:

"I stump you to hit *me*."

The stones soon began to fly promiscuously, and

the play grew more lively than safe. The boys became excited and ran in all directions, exclaiming "Hit *me*, hit *me!*" The missiles were dodged with exultant laughter, and the shots returned with interest.

As must be supposed, some of the players were really hit, and sore heads, and backs, and limbs made the sham skirmish before long a good deal like a real battle.

Belcher Whitmarsh was about the only really cool fellow on the ground.

"Come, fellows," he remonstrated, "this is getting dangerous. What's the good of throwing stones when you're mad? It's poor play, any way."

"Ho, you're afraid," shouted Roger Blake, and in this he was joined by several others.

Roger had received one rather hard thump, and feeling quite fiery about it determined to be "even with somebody." He kept on hurling right and left reckless of consequences.

Belcher paid no attention to the derision with which his words were treated. He was preparing, with one or two companions, to leave the playground when he saw Roger near him with a heavy stone in his hand drawing back for a furious throw.

Partly in sport and partly out of regard for the lad aimed at, he stepped behind the excited boy and caught his arm.

Roger whirled about instantly in a great heat. As Belcher stepped quickly backward, laughing, he let fly the stone at him with all his force, crying:

"Take it yourself, then!"

The stone struck Belcher full in the face, breaking two of his front teeth and knocking him down.

Seeing what he had done, Blake sobered in an instant and ran to the aid of his fallen schoolfellow.

"I didn't mean to, Belcher," said Roger, bending over him remorsefully, and evidently afraid he had killed him.

The boys began to express their indignation quite loudly, but Blake made no attempt to defend himself, only hanging over the injured lad, and declaring how sorry he was.

"Come," pleaded he, "try to get up, and let me help you down to the schoolhouse—I'll pay the doctor anything in the world to make you well again."

But Whitmarsh, as soon as he recovered a little, showed that he resented his sympathy as bitterly as he did his blow.

Pushing away his hand spitefully, he staggered to his feet with the help of another boy, and holding his handkerchief to his bloody face moved off the green, sobbing with pain and revengeful rage.

By the time school commenced he had been assisted to wash and bind up his bleeding mouth, when he started for home, giving Roger a look which was very seldom seen on his face, but which meant plainly enough:

"I'll have the worth of this out of your skin some day, see if I don't!"

That afternoon the boys received a sound lecture

from the teacher on the evil of throwing stones, and a penalty was imposed upon the leaders in the reckless sport, Roger among them, who, however, in consideration of his penitence, was only charged with a message to his parents, making full confession and submitting his case entirely to their judgment.

Days passed, and everything went on much as before at the school, save that Belcher Whitmarsh was missed, being at home healing his wound.

Every day that his absence was noticed was to Roger's quick feelings like a new condemnation.

No one was more pleased, then, than Roger Blake to see Belcher, after a little more than a week had passed, back at his place in school.

He soon found, however, that bygones were not to be bygones between them.

Belcher not only refused to respond to his hearty congratulations, but showed by his manner and words (hissed through his broken teeth) that so far from forgiving Roger's offense he meant to lay it up against him.

Several times when thrown in close company with him Blake tried to disarm his dislike.

"Come," he would say, "now, Belch, shake hands and say quits."

But Whitmarsh would only answer with a surly half threat, or grin significantly, to expose the notch in his gums where the teeth were gone.

The boys saw this unreasonable dislike, and gradually transferred their sympathy to Roger.

At last the school closed, and though Belcher was

not cordial the whole affair between the two lads seemed likely to be soon forgotten.

One day during vacation, as Roger was picking whortleberries with two other boys in a lonely pasture, he was unexpectedly joined by Belcher, who had come thither on the same errand.

It was not noticed that they greeted each other very differently from the usual manner of boys, and during the whole time they were together Belcher behaved himself in a way that made neither Blake nor his companions feel any the less at ease for his company. Least of all had they any reason to suspect that he still harbored his old revenge.

A ruined house, many years deserted, stood in sight of the spot where the boys were picking, and growing tired of their work they agreed to go and examine the old building, and perhaps take a game of "hi spy" there.

As they went over the house they found a trap-door opening into a small vault, which had evidently once been used for the family cellar—for the ancient dwelling was rather cramped in size and accommodations—and, boy-like, they all went down into the moldy hole.

As the last boy was descending the rotten ladder tumbled to pieces under his weight, and the adventurous youngsters found themselves caught like the fox and goat in the well.

Philip Granger, however, being a lad of quick resources, soon hit upon the fox's plan of getting out, which was that each should climb the shoulders of a comrade, and when all but one were safely above ground these should join in pulling out the last.

The plan was varied a little in practice, as it was awkward business to decide who of them should be the "goat."

Phil got up first, climbing over Frank Staples, and then aided his helper out.

Belcher, who had made a ladder of Roger Blake, was performing the pulling of his generous companion toward the opening, when a sudden yell was heard outside, and crying out "There come Dirk Avery and Ben Trench!" Frank and Phil darted away, running as if for their lives.

Seized with their panic, Belcher instantly dropped Roger, and regardless of his terrified calls rushed from the hut in a twinkling.

The jar of the hurried departure of the boys over the rickety floor brought down the trap-door with a bang, and Roger was left a prisoner indeed.

Dirk Avery and Ben Trench were two bad characters who lived a sort of half-vagabond life, rarely doing any honest work, and whose savage looks and cruel natures made them the terror of all the children of the neighborhood.

Their appearance in any place was the signal for a general stampede of the young people who happened to be about. There was not one in our little whortleberry party who was not as much afraid of them as if they had actually worn horns and hoofs.

On this occasion they were out on a fishing tramp, and the contents of a bottle of cheap rum that each of them carried had made them more wicked than usual.

Accordingly, they were in just the mood to take all possible advantage of the fright they had caused, and when the boys fled so precipitately from the ruined house they pursued them with horrible threats and shouts of hoarse laughter.

Frank and Phil ran toward the lot where they had hidden their baskets, the loud voice of Dirk crying, " Skin the rascals !   Wring their necks !"

Dirk, however, soon overdid himself, for the two boys were fleet of foot, and saved their breath. They finally got away, with their berries.

Belcher struck a bee-line for home, forgetting his basket, and though Ben gave him a hot chase he succeeded in distancing him.

Poor Roger ! For some minutes after he found himself shut fast in the vault his mortal fear of being found by the two roughs left him no courage to cry out, and gave him no time to think whether he ought to blame Belcher or not.

Judging his act by his own feelings then, he could not say but he should have done the same.

But the immediate fright soon passed, and he began to feel the real misery of his situation.

Nobody but Whitmarsh knew where he was. What if he *should* leave him there, for the old grudge ? And then it came to him how singular it was that the one on whom he depended to help him out should be just *he*—the boy who had threatened him.

Wearily enough passed the time to Roger down there in the dismal hole.

Neither shout nor scream would help him. No one lived within half a mile of the house; or if his cries should chance to be heard it might be Avery and Trench, and they would certainly bring him more hurt than good.

Suddenly he heard footsteps. A hand seized the trap-door and lifted it. Belcher Whitmarsh's face looked into the vault.

"Hollo," said Roger joyfully, "I thought you'd be back before long. Now let's get out of this—I've had enough of it, I'm sure."

But Belcher only grinned, showing the vacancy in his front teeth, and replied coolly:

"Want me to help you out?"

"Of course. Don't be fooling now," pleaded Roger.

"Well," said Belcher, "I've thought it over, and seeing you're in there so nicely *I've concluded I won't*. I've an old score against you. Perhaps you'd like to pay it now."

With that he dropped the trap-door, and made off.

He had come after his basket of berries. Would he be heartless enough to go home now and leave his schoolmate in that damp hole, pestilent with mildew and haunted, perhaps, by sliding adders and loathsome creatures?

Meantime the parents of Roger, when the hour passed at which he was expected home, began to make inquiries for him. Frank Staples and Philip Granger, who both supposed he had climbed out of the vault and ran away with Belcher from the hut, were much surprised when asked where he was, and told that he had not returned.

Their story of the encounter with Dirk Avery and Ben Trench made the parents still more anxious.

Possibly their boy had come to some harm at the hands of those drunken ruffians. Would Philip mind going over to the pasture again and showing just where it all happened?

Philip gladly consented, and getting leave from home accompanied Mr. Blake to the lot where they had gathered their berries.

Roger's basket was found untouched, precisely where he had been seen to hide it. Mr. Blake looked pale and Phil began to feel frightened.

"Let's go down to Mr. Whitmarsh's," said Mr. Blake, "and see Belcher."

It was now about sundown, but as the old house lay not far out of the way it was decided to visit it.

No sooner had they reached it and looked in than Phil exclaimed, "The trap-door is shut. I'm sure 'twas open when we left it."

In a moment more they had uncovered the vault and found poor Roger.

Overjoyed, they helped him out, a good deal the worse for the hunger and fear he had undergone.

The story of Belcher's mean revenge was soon noised abroad. He excused himself by saying he meant to leave Roger only a little while for a joke, but his father made him go to Mr. Blake's and apologize for his wanton trick.

We must do Belcher the justice to say that he performed the duty promptly and with apparent frankness and sincerity. There is no doubt, however, that he meant harm—not such serious harm as might have occurred—but sufficient injury to his playfellow to satisfy his malignant feelings and glut his revenge. The spirit he exhibited was the same in kind, although not in degree, as that which makes a man a murderer.

A true man never allows anger to get the permanent control of his feelings. He knows its mean and dangerous tendencies, and remembers the words of Him who spake as never man spake: "If ye forgive not men their trespasses, neither will your Father forgive your trespasses."

THE BOY IN THE BUSH.

"The impudent scoundrel! Just look at this, mamma. I should like to see him at it," exclaimed Sydney Lawson in great wrath, as he handed his mother a very dirty note which a shepherd had brought home. On coarse, crumpled grocer's paper these words were written in pencil:

"Master sidney i Want your Mare the chesnit with the white starr, soe You Send her to 3 Mile flat first thing Tomorrer Or i Shall Have to cum an Fetch Her. Warrigal."

"Sam says," Sydney went on to say, "that the fellow was coward enough to give it him just down by the slip-panels. He wouldn't have dared to talk about sticking us up if he hadn't known father was away. Send him my mare Venus! I seem to see myself doing it!"

Sidney Lawson, who made this indignant speech, was a tall, slim lad of fourteen. He and his mother had been left in charge of the station while his father took some cattle to Port Philip.

Sydney was very proud of his charge; he thought

himself a man now, and was very angry that Warrigal, a well-known desperado, should think he could be frightened " like a baby."

Warrigal was a bushranger who with one or two companions wandered about in that part of New South Wales, doing pretty much as he liked. They stopped the mail, and robbed draymen and horsemen on the road by the two and three dozen together. The police couldn't get hold of them.

The note that Sydney had received caused a great deal of excitement in the little station.

Miss Smith, who helped Mrs. Lawson in the house, and taught Sydney's sisters and his brother Harry, was in a great fright.

" Oh! pray send him the horse, Master Sydney," she cried, " or we shall all be murdered. You've got so many horses one can't make any difference."

Mrs. Lawson was as little disposed as Sydney to let Mr. Warrigal do as he liked. She knew that her husband would have run the risk of being " nabbed," if he had been at home, rather than have obeyed the bushranger's orders; and that he would be very pleased if they could manage to defy the rascal.

Still it was a serious matter to provoke Messrs. Warrigal & Co. to pay the house a visit. She felt sure that Sydney would fight and she meant to fire at the robbers herself if they came; but would she and Sydney be able to stand against three armed men?

Not a shepherd, or stockman, or horse-breaker

about the place was to be depended on; and Ki Li, the Chinaman cook, though a very good kind of fellow, would certainly go to bed in his hut if the robbers came by day, and stay in bed if the robbers came by night. John Jones, the plowman, whose wife was Mrs. Lawson's servant, slept in the house, and he was too honest to band with the bushrangers in any way; "but then, he's such a *sheep*, you know, mamma," said Sydney.

There was time to send word to the police in Jerry's Town; but who was to go?

Ki Li would be afraid to go out in the dark, and John Jones would be afraid to ride anything but one of the plow horses, and that only at an amble. It wouldn't do for Sydney to leave the place, since he was the only male on it who was to be depended upon, so what was to be done?

Little Harry had heard his mother and brother talking; and as soon as he made out their difficulty he looked up and said:

"Why, mamma, *I* can go. Syd, lend me your stock-whip and let me have Guardsman."

Neither mother nor brother had any fear about Harry's horsemanship, but they scarcely liked to turn the little fellow out for a long ride by night.

However, he knew the way well enough, and if he did not fall in with any of the Warrigal gang nobody would harm him.

So Sydney put the saddle and bridle on Guardsman and brought him round to the garden-gate, where Harry stood flicking about Sydney's stock-whip very impatiently, while his mamma kissed him and tied a comforter round his neck.

Harry shouted "Good-night," gave Guardsman his head, and was off like a wild boy.

Sydney stabled Venus, his favorite mare, and—an unusual precaution—turned the key in the rusty padlock; and when he had given a look about the outbuildings it was time for him to go in to supper and family prayers.

He read the chapter and Mrs. Lawson read the prayers. She was a brave woman, but with her little girls about her and her little boy away she couldn't keep her voice from trembling a little when she said, "Lighten our darkness, we beseech thee, O Lord; and by Thy great mercy defend us from all perils and dangers of this night."

Sydney went into his mother's bedroom and looked at the blunderbuss that stood by the bedhead (Mrs. Lawson had selected the blunderbuss as her weapon, because she thought she "must be sure to hit with that big thing") and he showed her once more how to pull the trigger.

Then he bade her "good-night," and went along the veranda to his own little room at one end, where he locked himself in, and drew the charge of his rifle and loaded it again, and looked at the chambers of his revolver, and put the caps on, and laid it down on a chair, ready to his hand.

When his preparations were completed he said his prayers and tumbled into bed with his clothes on.

Harry wasn't expected home until the next day. He had been told to sleep at the tavern in Jerry's Town, when he had left his message at the barracks, and come home at his leisure in the morning.

About four miles from Wonga-Wonga, the dreariest part of the road to Jerry's Town, begins a two-mile stretch of dismal scrub. Harry put his heels into Guardsman's sides to make him go even faster than he was going when they got into the scrub, and was pleased to hear a horse's hoofs coming toward him from the other end.

He thought it was a neighbor riding home to the next station; but it was Warrigal. As soon as Harry pulled up Guardsman to chat a minute, Warrigal laid hold of the bridle and pulled Harry on to the saddle before him.

"Let's see, you're one of the Wonga-Wonga" (that was the name of his father's station) "kids, ain't you?" said the robber. "And where are you off to this time of night? Oh, oh, to fetch the traps, I guess; but I'll put a stop to that little game."

Just then Harry gave a *coo-ey*. He couldn't give a very loud one, for he was lying on a sack on the robber's horse; but it made Warrigal very savage.

He put the the cold muzzle of a pistol against Harry's face and said, "You screech again, youngster, and you won't do it no more."

And then Warrigal took Harry and the horses into the scrub, and gagged Harry with a bit of iron he took out of his pocket, and tied him up to a crooked old honeysuckle-tree with a long piece of rope he carried in his saddle-bags.

"Don't frighten yourself, I'll tell yer mar where you are, and you'll be back by breakfast," said Warrigal, as he got on Guardsman and rode off, driving his own tired horse before him.

Next morning, just as the day was breaking, Warrigal and his two mates, with crape masks on, rode up to Wonga-Wonga.

They made as little noise as they could; but the dogs began to bark and woke Sydney.

When he woke, however, Warrigal had got his little window open, and was covering him with a pistol.

Sydney put out his hand for his revolver, and though Warrigal shouted, "Throw up your hands, boy, or I'll shoot you through the head," he jumped out of bed and fired.

He missed Warrigal, and Warrigal missed him; but Warrigal's bullet knocked Sydney's revolver out of his hand, and one of Warrigal's mates made a butt against the bedroom door and smashed it; and he and Warrigal rushed into the room, and threw Sydney down on the bed, and pinioned his arms with a sheet.

The other bushranger was watching the horses.

By this time the whole station was aroused. The men peeped out of their huts, half frightened, half amused; not one of them came near the house. John Jones and his wife piled their boxes against their room door, and then crept under the bed.

Miss Smith went into hysterics; and Gertrude and her sisters couldn't help looking as white as their night-dresses.

Mrs. Lawson had fired off her blunderbuss, but it had only broken two panes of the parlor window, and riddled the veranda posts; so Wonga-Wonga was at the bushrangers' mercy.

They ransacked the house, and took possession of any little plate, and jewelry, and other portable property they could find. When the robbers had packed up what they called the "swag," and put it on one of their horses, they pulled Ki Li out of bed, and made him light a fire, and cook some chops and boil some tea.

Then they marched Mrs. Lawson, and Miss Smith, and Sydney, and his sisters, and Mr. and Mrs. Jones, and Ki Li, into the keeping-room, and sat down to breakfast, with pistols in their belts, and pistols laid, like knives and forks, on the table.

The bushrangers tried to be funny, and pressed Mrs. Lawson and the other ladies to make themselves at home, and take a good meal. One of the robbers was going to kiss Miss Smith; but Sydney, pinioned as he was, ran at him, and butted him like a ram.

He was going to strike Sydney; but Gertrude ran between them, calling out, "Oh, you great coward!" and Warrigal felt ashamed, and told the man to sit down.

"We call him Politeful Bill," Warrigal remarked, in apology; "but he ain't much used to ladies' serciety."

When breakfast was over, Warrigal asked Sydney where the mare was.

"Find her yourself," said Sydney.

"Well, there won't be much trouble about that," answered Warrigal. "She's in the stable, I know; and you've locked her in, for I tried the door. I suppose you are too game to give up the key, my young fighting-cock? But since you're so sarcy, Master Sydney, you shall see me take your mare. You might as well ha' sent her instead of sending for the police, and then I shouldn't ha' got the bay horse too;" and he pointed to Guardsman, hung up on the veranda.

There was no time to ask what had become of Harry.

Warrigal hurried Sydney by the collar to the stable, while the other men mounted their horses, and unhooked Guardsman, to be ready for their captain.

Warrigal blew off the padlock with his pistol; but Venus was fractious, and wouldn't let him put on her halter. While he was dodging about the stable with her, Sydney heard hoofs in the distance. Nearer and nearer came the *tan-ta-ta-tan-ta-ta-tan-ta-ta*.

Four bluecoats galloped up to the slip-panels, three troopers and a sergeant; the sergeant with Harry on his saddlebow.

In a second Harry was down, and in three seconds the slip-panels were down too.

The waiting bushrangers saw the morning sun gleaming on their carbines, as the police dashed

between the aloes and the prickly pears, and letting
Guardsman go, were off like a shot.

Sydney banged to the stable door; and, setting
his back against it, shouted for help. His mother,
Gertrude, and even John Jones, as the police were
close at hand, ran to his aid; and up galloped the
troopers.

Warrigal fired a bullet or two through the door,
and talked very big about not being taken alive;
but he thought better of it, and in an hour's time
he was jogging off to Jerry's Town with handcuffs
on, and his legs tied under his horse's belly.

If Warrigal had not taken up little Harry, most
likely he would not have been caught; for when
Harry had got to Jerry's Town, he would have
found all the troopers away except one. In the
scrub, however, Harry heard the sergeant and his
men returning from a wild-goose chase they had
been sent on by the bush telegraphs; and managing
at last to spit the gag out of his mouth, he had given
a great *co-oo-oo-oo-oo-ey*.

After that night Miss Smith always called Sydney
Mr. Sydney; and Sydney let Harry ride Venus as
often as he liked.

THE MIDNIGHT RIDE.

It was half-a-dozen years before the war that Godfrey Brooks made a visit to his Cousin Sydney in Virginia. It was his first glimpse of plantation life, and he was not sparing of his questions or comments. Boys in a strange place find it hard to carry about with them the politeness or reticence which are such easy fitting garments at home.

The two boys were standing on the piazza one sunny morning looking down to the distant swamp.

"You mean to tell me," said Godfrey hotly, "that gentlemen hunted their runaway slaves out of the swamp with bloodhounds? Bloodhounds?"

"No, I don't. Gentlemen, of course, do no such dirty work. In the first place, our people (we don't call them slaves) never run away. Why, bless you, old Uncle Peter there, was a boy with my grandfather, and I'm sure I like him a deal better. Of all the hundreds of men and women my father owns, there's not one that don't respect and love him. But there's a class of whites who are not so respected, and when their people escape they bring them back —that's all."

"It's brutal," muttered Godfrey.

" A man has a right to reclaim his property," said Syd coolly.

Now neither of the boys knew much of the intrinsic merits of the question. They only echoed the words and arguments their elders threw back and forth unceasingly. When Syd began to give the details of the late hunt after a runaway horse-thief in the swamp, therefore, Godfrey's moral indignation cooled in the borrowed ardor of the chase.

"You see," Syd said in conclusion, "Boosey was really a criminal of the worst sort, as well as a slave, and he belonged to old Johnson. Johnson's the man that owns the hounds. That's his place beyond the hill. He's a whiskey distiller, and raises slaves for the market. Oh, of course he's tabooed. Even a decent laborer looks down on a man that raises slaves for the market."

The boys went out fishing presently, and Godfrey looked with a thrill of horror into the dark thicket of laurel and poisonous ivy as they passed where Boosey was still hidden. Down in his secret soul there was an idea of the fierce and terrible zest of hunting anything—even a man—with a bloodhound, through that tragic dusk and quagmire. It would be akin to the gladiatorial combats between man and beast of old Rome, or the bull-fights of the plaza, which his gentle Cousin Anne had learned to relish in Madrid.

" What do you say to riding over to Col. Page's to-night?" said Syd at supper. " The girls want to

practice some new music before the next party.
It's only six now. We can ride over in an hour."

"All right," said Godfrey.

"Remember, boys," said Dr. Brooks, "you are to
be at home and in bed by ten." For Syd's father,
while he bestowed horses, guns, every accessory to
pleasure upon his son with an unstinting hand, yet
held a tight rein on him and never allowed him to
fancy that he was a man and not in reality a child.

"We'll be home by ten, sir," the boys said
promptly.

Now Godfrey was but a schoolboy, and at home
only snubbed and kept in place by a half-dozen
grown brothers and sisters. This riding out at
night, therefore, on a pony, which for the time was
his own ; this calling on young ladies to whom he
was known as Mr. Brooks, of New York, was an
ecstatic taste of adult freedom which almost
intoxicated the boy. When nine o'clock came, and
Syd beckoned him from the sofa, where he was
reading "Locksley Hall" to Miss Amelia Page, he
rose so unwillingly as to cause Joe Page to look
from his game of backgammon.

"It's too bad in the doctor to put your cousin
into strict prison regulations, Syd," he said. "I'll go,
however, and see about your horses."

He came back with a queer twinkle in his eye.
"Sam declares he hitched them securely ; but
they're gone now. Sit down, boys, sit down. You
may as well make the best of it. The fellows are
after them. They'll be here by and by."

Syd looked annoyed. "I believe Joe unhitched them himself. I promised father I'd be back early." However he sat down quietly and waited. Godfrey had no annoyance to hide.

It wanted but ten minutes to eleven o'clock that night when the ponies were brought to the door, and the boys, after many hand-shakings and cordial invitations, were allowed to depart for home.

Then the glow of gallantry and manhood began to cool in Godfrey's bosom, and the unpleasant tremor to take its place which was wont to over-come him when he was late at school.

"I say, Syd, I wish we were at home," he said, mounting.

"I wish we were," gloomily.

"Will your father be very angry?"

"It isn't that. But I never broke my word to him before, never. I know what he thinks of a man that breaks his word. The road is heavy. It's a good ride for an hour and a half," shutting his watch with a snap.

"Is there no short cut?"

"Yes, there's one," looking at him dubiously; "but it's through Johnson's place."

"The dogs—they're not loose, eh?"

"That I don't know. He keeps them chained in daytime, of course, but whether the scoundrel looses them at night or not I never heard. It would be just like him."

The boys rode on in silence. Suddenly Syd drew up with a jerk. "Here's the gate into Johnson's, and

I tell you what it is I must go this way, dogs or no dogs. I'm in honor bound to try to keep my promise as nearly as I can, no matter what lies in the way. You can ride down the hill; I'll wait for you at the house."

"No, sir; I'm with you," feeling himself every inch a man at the chance of an adventure. "Open the gate, Syd. Now come on!" and giving their horses the rein they struck into a gallop down the road leading close by Johnson's house and stables. It was so heavily covered with tan-bark that the sound of the hoofs was deadened, and the boys spoke in whispers, afraid to stir the midnight silence.

Syd nodded toward a low kennel, back of the stables.

"There!" he motioned with his lips. "There's where they were when they took them to hunt Boosey."

But kennel and stables were silent and motionless in the cold moonlight.

The tan-bark was replaced by pebbles near the house. The boys took their ponies up on the short velvet turf, on which their swift feet fell with a crisp, soft thud, a noise hardly sufficient to rouse the most watchful dog, but which drove the blood from Godfrey's cheeks. His short-lived courage had oozed out.

"A man one could fight," he thought. "But to be throttled like a beast by a dog." The gladiatorial fights of Rome did not thrill him so much now as the thought of them had sometimes done.

Thud—thud. Every beat of the hoofs upon the grass sounded through the boys' brains. They were up to the kennels—past them—safe. Two minutes passed and not a sound. Godfrey drew a long breath, when—hark!

A long, deep bay, like thunder, sounded through the night.

"God save us! They're loose and are after us," gasped Syd.

Glancing back they saw two enormous black shapes darting from behind the shadow of the porch, and coming down the slope behind them.

"Now, Pitch and Tar!" sang out Syd, "it all rests on you." He shouted as cheerily, Godfrey thought, as though he were chasing a hare. Chasing and being chased were different matters, both the boys thought; though there was a reckless, gay defiance about the Southern boy which his cousin lacked, courageous as he was.

The ponies seemed to catch the meaning of Syd's call. They looked back. Their feet scarcely touched the sward, their nostrils were red, their eyes distended.

After the first fierce howl the dogs followed in silence. They had no time to give tongue; they had work to do.

A long stretch of pebbly road lay before the boys, then there was a thick patch of bushes, and beyond, the gate.

There was no doubt of the horses keeping up their pace. Terror served them for muscle and blood. But the hounds were swifter of foot at any time. They gained with every minute. The distance was about fifty yards.

"Can we do it?" Godfrey asked. His tongue was hot and parched.

"Of course we'll do it, unless the gate is locked."

After this new dread came they were silent. Godfrey thought of home, his mother, and poor little Nell; wished he had not snubbed her as he used to do.

Syd felt desperately in his pockets, where he found only a penknife. Why would not his father let him carry firearms as the other boys?

Suddenly turning to Godfrey he made a gesture, and turned his horse full on the hedge of privet. It leaped boldly—Godfrey's followed. But the hounds followed, relentless as fate, and dashed through the lower branches. They were closer than before.

"The gate! the gate!" cried Syd. He had reached it and fumbled for the bolt. Godfrey, a dozen paces behind, fancied he felt the tramp of the powerful beasts shake the ground. He turned, saw them coming with open jaws, closer, closer.

Would the gate never open? There was a creak and crash, and it rolled back on its rusty hinges. The horses darted through so violently as to throw Godfrey on the ground. When he looked up Syd was standing beside him, and from the other side of the iron bars came the baffled roar of the angry beasts.

The boys rode home without a word.

"What about reclaiming property by means of bloodhounds, Syd?" asked Godfrey.

"It's brutal," cried Syd vehemently, and then he laughed. "I tell you, Godfrey, one must actually take another man's place before he can be quite just to him, eh?"

A THOUSAND A YEAR.

"I am afraid Daniel must give up his studies," Mrs. Brooks said, sadly. "I've been thinking how we are to meet the expenses of another year, and it seems quite impossible to get money enough to do so."

"Oh, it would be such a pity, and brother so nearly through," Susan said, looking up in a distressed way. "He mustn't leave college now, when he is so near graduating! There *must* be a way of helping him through."

Mrs. Brooks stooped to kiss the pale, tender face upturned to hers.

"You have a wise little head, Susan, but I am afraid there is a problem here you cannot solve," said the widow, mournfully.

"How much will be needed?"

"At least a hundred dollars besides what he will earn himself. You know there are always extra expenses for the graduating class."

Susan's countenance fell. It was a great sum in her estimation, and it was already difficult for them to meet their weekly expenses.

"Everything depends upon brother's success,"

Susan said, presently. "We must give up every-thing for him."

"I cannot forget I have *two* children," the mother said, kissing the girl again more tenderly than before.

"Two children; but only one that will be a blessing to you," Susan said, brushing away a tear.

"Don't say that, Susie. I am proud of Daniel, I do not deny that—but I love you, too, all the same."

"But you never can be proud of me, weak and deformed as I am! Oh, mother, why are some flowers made so beautiful and fragrant, and some so dark and noisome? Why was my brother so fair, so talented, and I so repulsive?"

"No, no, no, not repulsive; don't say that," the widow cried, putting her arms around the girl in a sheltering way.

"Do you think Daniel will let me go to see him take his diploma, mother?"

"You would not be able, dear."

The girl laughed bitterly.

"No; brother would say I was not able, too. But I should be glad, so very glad to see him graduate. I think I would be willing to die then."

"Hush, my darling," the mother cried, with a sharp pain in her voice. "When you are gone I shall soon follow. Daniel will be satisfied with his laurels, but women—ah, my child—women must love something, and you are all that is left me to love."

Susan nestled her head in her mother's bosom

without speaking, and lay there so long that her mother thought she was sleeping. Suddenly she opened her eyes and said :

"I have thought it all out, mother. Daniel can graduate, and we will go see him take his diploma. Mr. Green needs girls to braid straw hats. You know I am nimble with my fingers, and I could braid a thousand a year, and that would be how much ?"

"But it would be wicked for me to allow you to overtask yourself in that way, darling. I am not sure but it might ruin your health, feeble as you are. No, no, it is not to be thought of."

"How many might I undertake, mother ?"

"Not half that amount; not a third, even."

"Would Daniel be willing for me to braid, do you think ?"

"I don't know. We will ask him."

"Mother," Susan said, looking into her eyes, "I believe this is my mission, to educate Daniel. You know we have given him everything—my portion of the property and yours. I think I could hold out to do this last, and you will consent when you come to reflect upon what it will be to brother, and to you, when I am gone. But he must not know it. It would wound his pride, and he would get some false notion in his head that he could not use money I had earned in that way. Now, promise me, that let what will come, you will never tell him that I braided straw hats that he might complete his education."

"I cannot promise *never* to tell him, darling, because I cannot foresee the future, but I should not like him to be humbled and wounded, more than yourself. I am too old to learn readily, but perhaps I, too, could earn something by braiding."

The determination was now fully settled in the mind of each, that the young man must graduate, and that the bills must be met by them. The patronage of Mr. Green was solicited, and it was agreed the work should be taken home, and that a thousand hats should be braided for ten cents each, which he assured them was more than he would think of paying to any one else, and only to Susan in consideration of her infirmity.

We ought, perhaps, to explain that Susan had been early afflicted with a curvature of the spine, which had sadly deformed her. She would never have been a beautiful girl, Daniel having inherited not only all the family talent, but its beauty as well. But her eyes were wondrously attractive, with their loving, yearning persuasiveness, and few could remember her deformity who had felt the warmth of her generous nature.

In due time, the anticipated letter of inquiry came from Daniel, asking what the prospects were for the coming year. It was full of dismal forebodings and egotistical complaints of the hard fortune that made him dependent upon his mother, but there was no regret that she suffered too; no longing to be a man that he might take this lonely couple in his strong arms and bear them tenderly over the rough places of life; only vague, ambitious dreamings of what he was to be to the world, and the world to him.

The widow laid down the letter with a sigh. Susan read the pages over and over again. So grounded was she in her love for this earthly idol that the selfishness was less apparent to her than to her mother.

Its sadness seemed like tenderness, and he could not speak too often or too much of the genius which she believed he possessed, and which would some time break upon the world like the meteor to which he rather tritely compared himself.

"Ah, we shall be so proud of him!" Susan said, folding the letter and laying it away near her heart, where it rested many and many a day, while she wove the strands of straw in and out, thinking how ten times ten made one dollar, and how the dollars would some time count up to a hundred, and that sum, which her fingers had wrought out, would save her brother from discouragement, if not from despair.

The first twenty-five dollars was earned, and the money was sent the brother.

"He was very glad of it," he said. "He had begun to fear lest they would fail him." There was no inquiry how it had been obtained; no solicitude lest those who loved him had deprived themselves of luxuries, perhaps necessities, to meet his demands.

The next twenty-five dollars was earned, with greater difficulty. The widow was awkward at braiding, and her work unsatisfactory, and so some of it was returned to Susan. She sat up later nights, that her mother should not see how hard the work pressed upon her; but the twenty-five dollars came at last, and was sent to the student. Then there was another letter of thanks.

"If you would but rest, darling," the mother would say, when some look more wan than another startled her into keener anxiety.

"When it is done we will rest together," was all the reply the solicitude brought.

It was too late to retract now, the mother thought; and Daniel so nearly through! So they pinched a little from their daily meals, a little from the store of candles, a little from the evening fire, and prayed that every penny might be multiplied like the widow's meal.

One night Mrs. Brooks had gone to bed exhausted and hysterical with overlabor. Susan pressed the blankets tenderly around her mother's shoulders, and having given her the good-night kiss, and quieted her with many promises of soon following her, she went back to the kitchen fire and resumed the weary braiding.

She had not completed her usual task that week, and the idea occurred to her that her mother having fallen asleep, she could braid another hat before retiring. So she set up new strands and the thin fingers wove them patiently in and out, until sharp pain clutched her with merciless teeth, and she leaned forward, her head falling upon the table, in a dead faint.

It was long past midnight when Susan found herself in this position. Shivering with cold, she crept to her mother's side and lay the remainder of the night, racked by alternate fevers and chills.

How could the poor child tell her mother of what she knew was creeping so steadily toward her? Would she make a final effort to save her own life and let Daniel struggle with his fortunes as he best could?

Poor, brave little heart, with the chill of the grave stealing over it, but warmed back into life and renewed suffering by the wonderful strength of its undying love!

Another twenty five dollars was forwarded to Daniel, and a few lines came flying back by the return post, for Daniel was a man of business habits, and punctual in all things.

Susan looked it all over carefully for some loving message to her; some sign answering to what she felt in her own heart toward him, but there was nothing there but " *With love to Susan, I remain, etc., Daniel.*"

A dry sob escaped the poor child as she laid it by, and took up the weary, rustling braids. The sound rasped upon her nerves now. The very odor of the strands nauseated her. Every kink in the braids fretted her; and when one hat was finished and laid aside, it seemed such a mountainous task to commence another.

Sometimes hours would pass by without a round being accomplished, then again the nimble fingers would be inspired, and the work would grow as of old.

"If I could only go and see Daniel take his diploma," she would say, I think it would make me strong again. I would wear my white muslin frock, with the blue sash, and he would not be ashamed of me."

But it was not to be. The one thousand hats were braided, and Susan's task was done. Nothing remained for her but to lie down in her modest casket and sleep with folded hands until the blessed Saviour shall bid her approach to receive His welcome—"Well done, thou good and faithful servant."

Daniel returned with his collegiate honors only to listen to the sad story of her labors and death. His mother told it as they stood by the coffin. There were the worn letters she had cherished, blistered all over with tears.

He was conscience stricken when he looked them over, and saw how cold and egotistical they were, and how thoughtless he had always been of the treasure that death had taken. He took the thin hands in his—the hands that had braided and plaited while he slept, and wrought out the treasure-trove that molded the key to his success, and he made solemn resolutions for the future. Let us hope that, in her broken life, he learned how beautiful in the sight of God and angels is the self-sacrifice of the lowly in heart: and how much better it is to die in the struggle to bless others than it is to live to a selfish, unloving, unsanctified old age.

THE END.